Compass of Secrets

A Primrose Eversley Mystery
Book 1

A bookish whodunit with a librarian sleuth, ancient artifact, and secrets hidden behind locked doors.

Raynie Taylor

Compass of Secrets

Library of Congress Control Number: 2025927803

ISBN Paperback: 979-8-9923669-6-9
ISBN eBook: 979-8-9923669-7-6

First Edition

Published in the United States of America by RLA Publishing.

For more information, or to book an event, contact:
Bookings@raynietaylor.com
https://www.raynietaylor.com

Book and cover design by RLA Publishing

The Amazon Endure typeface was designed by 2K/DENMARK in 2025.Template id: ST-414D415A-25-A

For Sallie

CAST OF CHARACTERS

Primrose Eversley–A 33-year-old American librarian and archivist who inherits her late father's antique bookshop located in early 1900s Haworth, England; she discovers the bookshop is more than it seems.

Alaric Eversley–Primrose's estranged father; an archeologist and owner of a shop housing rare books and artifacts from around the world.

Athena–Alaric's loyal companion, ever watchful from the shadows, keeper of secrets, and keen at seeing what others cannot.

Rowan Ashcroft–A charming journalist with a quick wit and a knack for uncovering stories others would rather keep hidden. His resourcefulness and enigmatic air make him both an ally and a mystery in his own right.

Maggie Thistle–A bright and enthusiastic young apprentice at the bookshop, whose eagerness to help often leads her to stumble upon details others overlook.

Dr. Thaddeus Bellamy–An archaeologist and trusted colleague of Alaric Eversley, whose knowledge of history and ancient artifacts often proves invaluable.

Father Elias Hargrave–The town's reserved parson, respected for his guidance and knowledge, though his motives are not always as clear as his sermons.

Harold Fenwick–A well-connected merchant with influence in local affairs, whose polished manners conceal deeper ambitions.

PROLOGUE

He sat alone in his study; the night gathered cold and tight against the windows. For a moment he watched the fire as it danced in the hearth, warming the room.

Flame light climbed the walls in slow, dappled waves, gilding the spines of the books on the shelves and catching on the metal corners of frames that had remained unmoved for years. The room smelled of leather softened by time—and beneath it all, something sharp and clean, an evergreen harvested late this summer, rosemary; ever so faint, as if memory.

In his hand, a pen—gold and ebony—rested like a relic. He did not write quickly. There was no haste in him now, only certainty.

He had stumbled upon something he shouldn't have. How could he have been so careless?

The paper that lay before him was thick, costly, and chosen not for beauty but for strength. He stared at the blank space a moment longer than necessary, as if willing the words to arrange themselves into something that could erase years of regret.

At last, he began.

The scratching of the nib was the only sound in the room, steady and measured. His hand did not tremble—not until he reached the line he had dreaded most.

"Oh, how I love you, my sweet girl."

He paused there, the ink dark and honest on the page, and for a moment the fire seemed to quiet, as if the house itself were listening. If he could have seen her just once more—if he could have heard her voice in the doorway, even sharp with old hurt—it would have made something in him ease. It would have made the world feel less final.

But finality had arrived all the same.

When he finished, he signed his salutation with the same care he used when handling rare editions. He folded the letter once, twice—edges aligned, creases clean—and slid it into an envelope the color of bone.

Then came the seal.

He warmed the wax, watched it soften and pool, then pressed his sigil into it as he had so many times. The crest caught the firelight when he lifted it away— sharp lines, ancient intention—and the wax held that faint herbal scent as though it symbolized the very act of goodbye.

Outside, the cold pressed closer. Indeed, it was unusually cold and drizzly for the end of summer in Haworth, England.

The silence broke with a sound that did not belong: the squeal of wood on metal; the scraping of carriage brakes. Typical during the day on the downhill slope of Haworth's cobbled Main Street, but not this late in the night.

His gaze lifted, not startled—only resigned.

Across the desk, Athena watched him intently. For ten years she had been his quiet companion, a presence that asked nothing of him and understood more than anyone ever had.

He leaned toward her and whispered, so that the words would not carry.

A secret.

One he knew she would keep.

"Go now," he murmured. "And do not let yourself be seen."

He held up the envelope. She took it with solemn precision, as if she understood what it meant to hold a person's last hope.

He stood up from his desk slowly and put on his jacket. His pocket held the other item he could not leave to chance.

He drew it out—a compass, bejeweled and heavy in his palm. It caught the fire's light and threw it back in tiny starbursts—dark stones, bright facets, a needle that never sat entirely still.

He exhaled; the sound caught somewhere between a sigh and a prayer.

2

"Take care of my girl," he said, not to Athena alone, but to the compass itself, as if it were capable of loyalty.

Then, he crossed the room to the bookcase.

A lifetime of work lived there: rare tomes from antiquity, obscure pamphlets, first editions acquired through patience and sacrifice. His fingertips lingered on a familiar spine before he withdrew a worn, treasured copy of Emily Brontë's *Wuthering Heights*, published under the pen name Ellis Bell.

Behind it, hidden in the shelf's shadow, was a compartment no casual eye would ever find.

He placed the compass inside.

For a moment he held his hand there, then he slid the book back into place.

He turned and walked out toward the stairs.

Athena remained in the shadows, the envelope secured. He looked at her once more, just once—his gaze steady.

His steps were heavy as he began his descent. The spiral wooden staircase curled downward through the shop silent but with a memory, as though it remembered every person who'd ever hesitated here.

By the fifth step, the upstairs felt impossibly far away, and his weathered hands found the rail, gripping as though it could anchor him to the living world a moment longer.

At the bottom of the stairs, he reached for his scarf and hat from the antique hall tree. He lifted his spectacles, cleaned them with a cloth that had seen years of use, and placed them back upon his nose.

His lips moved, making barely a sound. "What these eyes have seen... God help me."

At the front door of the shop, he paused.

Outside, another sound—closer now.

Footsteps.

The familiar click of a cane hitting cobblestone. The subtle impatience of men who believed they had already won.

When he opened it, cold rushed in like a wave, and the shop's bell gave an eerie toll.

Two familiar faces stood on the threshold, their coats dark against the dim street. They smiled with the careful ease of men who knew precisely how far politeness could stretch before it snapped. The man in the top hat nodded and said in a gruff voice, "Alaric."

Alaric returned the nod because he had always been a courteous man.

The tension between them thickened, filling the doorway, pressing into the silence.

Alaric's eyes widened as he drew a breath.

And then—

A brief, bright burst: yellow-orange, sharp as lightning at close range.

The .455 Webley spoke once, and the sound cracked the night open.

In the shadows above, Athena did not move. But her eyes fixed on the man in the hat—recognition.

She backed away without a sound, deeper into the dark, taking the letter with her.

Keeping the secret.

1 THE INHERITANCE

A circle of glass enlarged her hazel eye as Primrose bent over the worn leather binding. Through the lens, the delicate cracks in the spine seemed like ancient rivers, branching across the surface of a forgotten map. Her hands, steady and sure, coaxed the fragile thread through the page's seam, tightening the stitch with the patience of a woman accustomed to repairing more than just paper.

The Astor Library's archives lay hushed around her, its towering shelves of books encompass her and rise like sentinels in the fading afternoon light. The scent of leather, dust, and ink clung to the air. The library was the realized vision of the richest man in New York, John Jacob Astor, although he would never see it himself. Free public libraries didn't exist in New York prior to this, and Primrose jumped at the opportunity to work in the archives.

She paused, fingertips brushing the margin of a manuscript so old the ink had paled to a ghostly brown. There was something about the work they were restoring—something that pressed at the edge of her thoughts like an unanswered riddle. She adjusted her spectacles, brushed a curl from her cheek, and bent closer in the quiet ritual of repair.

Somewhere beyond the great arched windows, carriage wheels clattered and the city stirred. Autumn had arrived with purpose. The cool, dry wind tugged at hat brims and rustled the amber leaves that danced along Lafayette Street. Gas lamps flickered to life against a sky that was just beginning to blush with twilight. But here—in this quiet corner—Primrose Eversley's world narrowed to parchment and paste.

Outside, the Astor Library rose from the East Village

like a monument to thought itself with its rust-red sandstone and brick facade. It stood quiet and regal, framed by wrought iron fencing and a pair of ornate lampposts.

A young man approached, his footsteps crisp and measured.

He wore a finely cut wool coat in charcoal gray, double-breasted with a pewter clasp at the waist. A plaid scarf of deep burgundy and ash blue wrapped neatly at his collar, and dark gloves covered his hands. His features, sharply defined, and clean-shaven. Eyes the shade of a summer sky, studied the building with an intensity that seemed too alert for someone so young.

His boots—polished but worn—struck the stone steps with a rhythmic certainty. At the top, he paused, removed his cap, and let the autumn wind tousle his sandy blonde hair before pulling open the heavy wooden door.

The hush inside was near sacred.

Brass sconces cast golden light across high-beamed ceilings and the curves of arched alcoves. Shelves of dark mahogany towered around him, holding volumes bound in weathered leather and gold leaf. A long reading table stretched beneath a central skylight, where the last of the sunlight poured in like a blessing. A faint scent of beeswax, polish, and old parchment drifted in the air, bringing a slight smile to the young man's face.

He removed his gloves, tucked them carefully into his coat, and stepped forward.

He wasn't here for pleasure or study.

He was here with a purpose.

He crossed the marble tiled floor to the librarian's desk, where a matronly woman peered at him over her spectacles. Without waiting to be greeted, he placed a sealed envelope on the polished wood and gave a polite nod.

"Please ensure this reaches Miss Primrose Eversley at her earliest convenience."

Before she could respond, he turned and strode out, vanishing into the fading light like a figure from a forgotten story.

The librarian squinted after the young man as the heavy door whispered shut behind him. She studied the envelope for a moment. It was a thick piece of paper, sealed with wax in a foreign crest. She rose from her desk with the weighty grace of someone used to moving through silence.

Her low heels clicked softly across the marble as she wound her way past reading rooms and side alcoves. The quiet hush of the library enveloped her, broken only by the occasional rustle of pages or the metallic whisper of a cart being wheeled through a far aisle.

She descended a narrow staircase, lit by amber sconces and softened by the hush of time. The air grew cooler as she passed through a stone archway into the archives—a quieter world tucked beneath the public floors, where the curious and the scholarly often lost track of time.

Here, the walls were lined with rolling ladders and ceiling-high shelves of uncatalogued tomes, vellum-bound manuscripts, and half-restored volumes awaiting attention. Ink bottles, bone folders, brushes, and book presses were arranged neatly on long worktables, their purpose known only to the initiated.

She found Primrose Eversley exactly where she expected: hunched over a padded cradle holding a rare edition of *The Grete Herball*. The book's cracked leather cover spread open like the wings of a tired bird.

Footsteps echoed in the room—crisp, deliberate, drawing nearer. Primrose did not look up at once. Whoever it was could wait; she had learned long ago that books carried more urgency than people suspected. Still, the sound tugged at her concentration forcing her to acknowledge it. She paused with the needle poised in midair.

"You can't just use gum arabic and call it restored," Primrose was saying, her voice soft but certain. "This binding is pre-industrial. You'd strip the original character entirely. What it needs is a boiled starch paste—see how the leather's delaminated from the board?"

The young man beside her, a fellow archivist named Henri, looked sheepish, holding a brush like a guilty schoolboy. He nodded as she lifted the edge of the binding with delicate precision, revealing the brittle thread beneath.

Primrose Eversley was not a striking woman in the traditional sense, but in this world of whispering pages

3

and centuries-old dust, she was magnetic. Brunette curls were pinned in a modest updo, a wisp or two escaping to frame her hazel eyes. Her dress, simple but smart, bore ink stains at the cuff—unnoticed or unbothered by it.

The head librarian cleared her throat softly.

Primrose glanced up, lips parting in the faintest smile. "Oh, Mrs. Hollingsworth. Hello."

"I've something for you, Miss Eversley." She held out the envelope like it was made of porcelain. "Delivered by hand. A young man—didn't leave his name."

Primrose set her needle down and wiped her fingers carefully on her apron before accepting it. Her brow furrowed as she turned the envelope over. The wax seal caught the light, shimmering faintly revealing a crest she didn't recognize.

"Strange," she murmured. "It smells like..."

She paused. "Rosemary."

Henri blinked. "That's... oddly specific."

But Primrose didn't answer. She was already reaching for the letter opener on the table, the scent of the herb stirring something long buried.

Not a memory.

A warning, heartbreak.

Primrose excused herself with a polite nod, her fingers curling gently around the envelope as she stepped away from the worktable. She didn't stray far, just past a row of narrow shelves to a quiet alcove lined with poetry and private histories. Here, the filtered light from a small, paned window fell in slanted beams across the floor, catching the fine dust that danced in the still air.

The quiet was different here. Not the orchestrated silence of the archives, but the intimate hush of things forgotten.

She paused beside an armchair tucked between shelves, the scent of rosemary rising as she lifted the envelope once more. It was faint, but distinct. The smell caught her off guard, sudden and intrusive.

Her throat suddenly dry made her swallow hard.

The paper was thick and heavy, an expensive blend, the kind chosen for importance. The wax seal was still intact, and she traced it absently with her thumb. The texture reminded her of the spine of an uncut volume: resistant, yet fragile.

She opened the flap with her letter opener—slowly, deliberately—and unfolded the thick parchment inside.

Her eyes skimmed the handwriting. It was elegant, slanted, and unmistakably English.

And though she read silently, the words echoed in the chamber of her mind, as if spoken aloud in her own careful voice, each syllable shaped by her upbringing, her education, her restraint.

"Miss Primrose Eversley,

It is with regret that I must inform you of the passing of your father, Mr. Alaric Eversley of Haworth, West Yorkshire, on the evening of the thirtieth of August, in the year of our Lord 1901.

Per the terms of his final testament, you have been named the sole inheritor of his estate, including the premises and contents of Eversley's Books and Curiosities, located on Main Street, Haworth."

She inhaled—shallow, then steadied. Her hand trembled, just once.

"You are requested to arrange for travel to Haworth at your earliest convenience. Further instructions and the key to the premises will be provided upon your arrival.

Respectfully,
Ambrose Withers, Solicitor
Leeds & County Chambers, Yorkshire."

She lowered the letter to her lap, fingers still pressed to the edge of the parchment, as if releasing her grip would cause her to lose any hope she had left.

The scent of rosemary clung to the fibers like a memory pressed between pages—bright and bitter, the way dried herbs release their essence long after life has left them. It stirred something quiet and unsteady inside her. Something she did not care to name.

A breath caught in her throat—not grief, exactly. More like the ache of a puzzle left unsolved.

He has died.

The phrase formed in her mind not with drama, but with the quiet finality of a closing book. No tearful revelation, no gasping sorrow—just a stillness. A weight.

Twenty-two years, and not a single word. And now, an entire estate.

She brushed her thumb over the wax seal again, as if doing so might summon some lingering trace of his intentions.

She murmured.

She raised her head toward the window, gaze unfocused.

"It was his world. Mysterious. Solitary. Always just beyond my reach." she said spitefully. *"And now, he offers it to me. Not in conversation. Not in apology. But in inheritance."*

She paused, as the rosemary laced the air again.

"Perhaps this is all he had left to give." she murmured again.

She sat for a long moment in silence, the letter resting open in her lap.

No sound reached her but the distant shush of paper being turned. Even the air seemed to pause; it was still and reverent.

Her hands, now steady, gripped the edges of the letter once more. And then, slowly, her composure faltered.

One tear escaped—quietly, unceremoniously— tracing a soft path down her cheek before she brushed it away with the back of her wrist. Not out of shame, but from habit. Emotion, after all, was best kept tidy.

She folded the letter with care and pressed it to her chest, her breath catching in a long, slow sigh.

"Goodbye, then," she whispered, not knowing if she meant the past, the man, or the certainty she had carried until this moment.

Then, composed once more, she stood.

The familiar rhythm of the library returned to her ears—the soft scrape of chairs, the quiet murmur of Henri speaking to Mrs. Hollingsworth. The scent of beeswax and vellum.

Primrose stepped lightly into the room, her hands folded neatly before her, the envelope now tucked into her coat.

"Forgive the interruption," she said gently. "I've just

received news. My father has passed away."

There was a pause. Henri, who had been pretending to fuss with the binding, looked up at her words. His face softened, as though unsure whether to offer condolence or remain silent. He chose silence, which Primrose found she preferred.

"I shall need to return to England at once. Haworth, to be specific."

Mrs. Hollingsworth's brows lifted with soft concern. She offered a faint, composed smile, the kind meant to reassure others when one hasn't quite managed to reassure oneself.

"I trust the archives will carry on without me for a time." And with that Primrose gathered her things and turned to leave.

By the time she stepped outside, the lamps had been lit. Their golden halos flickered gently against the deepening blue of twilight, and the air had turned crisp with the promise of an early frost.

Primrose wrapped her scarf more tightly around her neck and turned northward, her boots tapping a steady rhythm against the pavement. The city pulsed softly around her—shopkeepers drawing down awnings, carriage wheels clattering, the distant sound of a violin from an open window. Life continuing, unaware of her hidden heartbreak.

She walked with purpose, though her thoughts wandered.

Two days, perhaps three, to prepare.

She had always found comfort in structure. And so, as the wind tugged at the corners of her coat and leaves rustled at her feet, her mind began its quiet, orderly work. List-making steadied her nerves—it brought shape to uncertainty.

"Arrange for passage. The Cunard or White Star line, whichever is quickest. Preferably a single berth."

"Withdraw funds from the Barclay's account."

"Notify Mrs. Hollingsworth and draft a formal letter of leave for the archives board."

"Pack for sea travel—modest but respectable attire. Good walking boots."

"Retrieve Father's letters from the cedar box beneath the wardrobe."

She paused at a corner, watching as a hansom cab passed. Its solitary horse snorting steam into the cold air, while the driver—perched high behind—tugged at the reins with practiced ease. The cab's black body rocked slightly as it turned the corner, its curved roof gleaming under the gaslight.

"*Secure travel papers. Bookshop keys to be collected from the solicitor. Ambrose Withers, Leeds.*"

"*Determine estate condition. Inventory contents. Assess personal items.*"

"*Mind emotional composure throughout.*"

That last item appeared unbidden, but she did not remove it. Instead, she tucked the letter closer beneath her coat, where the scent of rosemary could not intrude and distract her.

"*And pack a copy of Whitman. For the journey.*"

She exhaled softly, her breath curling in the cool air.

Yes. There was much to do. But lists made even the most uncertain paths walkable.

Primrose Eversley crossed the final street toward home, the gas lamps flickering gently behind her.

And somewhere, across the ocean, the past waited.

2 THE VOYAGE

The sea was not cruel, but it was relentless.

Each wave rose and fell, lapping against the hull of the steamship with the rhythm of breath—eternal, and unmoved by the comings and goings of its passengers.

Primrose stood on the second-class promenade deck, a narrow walkway that curved discreetly along the midsection of the vessel. The wind teased at her scarf, tugged at the hem of her wool skirt, and brought with it the scent of the ocean, smoke, and distant rain.

After more than ten days at sea, she had become accustomed to ship's intricacies.

Her gloves, though simple and worn at the seams, were clean. Her coat—charcoal-gray, lined modestly— fit snugly across her curvy frame, tailored to suggest dignity rather than excess. She wore it like armor, every button fastened, every fold exact. There was elegance in her restraint, a beauty not declared but quietly held.

She had packed it herself, along with a sturdy travel trunk and a canvas satchel filled with carefully selected books and correspondence.

She had already begun a new page in her travel journal that morning, and now she skimmed through her writing looking for a page to continue her thoughts. *Day One. Departure completed without difficulty. Second-class berth satisfactory. Seas mild.*

She paused, then read a few more before finding the day's entry. *"It's easy to lose track of the days at sea. It's been thirteen days and tomorrow we shall arrive at Liverpool, England."* As she picked up where she left off, she glanced occasionally at her surroundings, ever observant of what she sees.

Around her, fellow second-class passengers paced or leaned quietly along the rail. A middle-aged woman was knitting at a bench in the fading light. A cluster of German-speaking students played cards. A red-cheeked gentleman struggled to light a pipe that kept blowing out in the wind.

Primrose took it all in without intrusion.

A steward passed, pushing a wooden tea trolley with chipped porcelain cups and small buttered scones wrapped in linen. She accepted a cup with a quiet thank you, dipping her chin politely before retreating once more to the bench near the rail.

Tea warm. Palatable. Appetite minimal. Emotional state... watchful.

The steamship surged forward through the gray-blue water, bound for Liverpool. Beyond that—Haworth and a bookshop she hadn't seen since childhood. A father-daughter relationship buried in unfamiliar soil.

She was distracted momentarily by a child making faces at her from behind his mother's overskirt. His small scrunched up face came into focus and made her laugh loudly. She looked around and quickly made a face back before regaining her composure.

She reached into her coat pocket and felt for the letter. The paper was soft now, worn from rereading, the scent of rosemary all but faded.

"Upon arrival: confirm solicitor appointment. Secure lodging. Inspect estate."

"No dramatics. No indulgence. Sadness and longing still. Push it aside."

Her handwriting had grown tighter over the years—more controlled, less romantic.

"And do not imagine what cannot be recovered."

A gull circled low over the railing, its cry sharp against the dull sky. The sea, ever moving, stretched endlessly ahead.

Primrose brought the teacup to her lips, breathing in the steam. The wind bit her cheek, but she sat still.

"Alaric Eversley." She sighed.

Primrose had grown restless after dinner. The rhythm of the sea, steady though it was, left her thoughts circling like gulls above a tide. She slipped a shawl across her shoulders and made her way down the corridor, following the glowing sconces and the faint promise of warmth.

The reading room lay toward the stern, tucked between the gentlemen's lounge and the writing salon. She finished her copy of Whitman's *Leaves of Grass* days ago. A steward opened the carved mahogany door for her, and she smiled as she entered. The hush within fell around her like a quilt.

It was an intimate chamber, paneled in dark oak and softened by velvet drapes with the color of burgundy wine. A row of bookcases lined the far wall, their spines gleaming in gold and green. At the center stood a hearth, its carved mantel crowned with a clock that ticked in time with the pulse of the engines below. Flames licked quietly at the logs, throwing out a glow that gilded the room in shifting amber.

She drew in a breath—woodsmoke, leather, and something else.

Rosemary.

It lingered faint and sharp beneath the warmth of the fire. Her brow furrowed, but she allowed herself a small smile. Perhaps the kitchen lies just beyond, she thought. Or a cook has been careless with his herbs.

Her gaze drifted over the shelves until it found a familiar name. "Mr. Charles Dickens." She said as she drew out a copy of Great Expectations, its cover worn soft by other hands. She carried it to a green leather armchair near the hearth. The fire crackled, a comfortable sound, yet her eyes kept straying from the page in fits of distraction.

From the corner of her vision, the flames seemed to shift—not merely upward, but curling sideways, spiraling in small, deliberate whorls. She blinked, looked fully at the fire as it danced innocently, logs collapsing into embers. She returned her gaze to the book, only for the flicker to tug again at her attention.

This time she caught it—a brief spiral, flame curling inward as though drawn toward an unseen center, before unraveling into the ordinary scatter of sparks. It was gone as quickly as it had come, leaving only the pop of sap and the perfume of rosemary in its wake.

She looked around the room and no one else seemed to have noticed. There was an elderly man in the leather chair by the door. He had a beard and was smoking a pipe; lost in the news of the world. A woman and two children sitting on the velvet couch on the far wall reading quietly the fairy tales of Hans Christian

Andersen. And a woman sitting at a table with her tea probably getting lost in the genteel poverty at the Orchard House of *Little Women*.

Primrose pressed closed the book she had in her lap. The spine creaked, but her thoughts were elsewhere. A spiral of fire. A scent from her childhood. *Coincidence?* She thought.

She sat very still, telling herself it was nothing more than the trick of tired eyes and shifting air.

The sea had darkened into indigo by the time Primrose made her way below deck, the teacup long forgotten, the last entry in her journal written with a precise but slanted hand.

The second-class corridor was narrow, lit with lanterns. Wood paneling lined the walls—warm in color but worn by salt and time.

Her cabin—B-217—was tucked near the end of the hall. She unlocked the door and stepped inside, closing it softly behind her.

It was small, but tidy.

A single narrow bed pressed against the far wall. A washbasin stood beside a cabinet of polished oak. Above it, a small mirror framed in bronze showed her reflection in the low light, windblown, pale, thoughtful. A desk folded down from the wall, just large enough for her journal and fountain pen. Her trunk sat obediently at the foot of the bed.

She unfastened her coat and scarf, draping them carefully on the peg by the door. The stillness of the cabin pressed in around her, intimate but not unkind. It reminded her of old confessionals: quiet places meant for private reckonings.

She sat on the edge of the bed and removed her boots, then pulled a wool shawl from the trunk and wrapped it around her shoulders. Her fingers brushed against something beneath the shawl—a letter—not the solicitor's, but another one. Older. Unopened.

She paused. Her heart quickening.

It was addressed in her father's hand.

She didn't remember packing it. In truth, she hadn't seen it in years. And now she could feel her face getting warm and her eyes welling up.

"How did this find its way into my trunk?"

Her fingers lingered on the faded ink. She didn't open it. Not yet. Some truths were best met with a clear head and a steady heart.

She placed it gently in the drawer of the washstand and turned the small lock.

Outside, the ship groaned quietly, its steel frame responding to the shifting sea. Pipes creaked overhead. Somewhere down the corridor, a man coughed in his sleep.

Primrose folded back the quilt and settled onto the mattress, the bed dipping slightly under her weight. She tucked the shawl tighter around her shoulders and stared at the ceiling for a long while.

"A letter I do not remember. A scent I have not smelled in years. A shop full of books I've never read."

She closed her eyes.

And as the ship rocked gently beneath her, she dreamed not of the sea, but of locked doors.

And keys that no longer turned.

Primrose had spent two weeks at sea when finally, the ship moaned against the dock as its ropes were secured, jolting Primrose from a half-sleep.

She rose slowly from her bunk, smoothing her shawl and brushing her hair into a modest twist. Her trunk was ready to be retrieved, her gloves laid out neatly on top of it. The room already felt impersonal again.

She gave the cabin a final sweep of her eyes, her gaze lingering on the empty washbasin—and the small drawer she'd forgotten.

She hesitated.

Then opened it.

The letter still lay inside, exactly where she'd placed it, the edges slightly curled from the dampness of being at sea. For a moment, she simply stared at it, the way one might glance back at a house locked for the last time.

Primrose slipped it into her satchel.

Outside, the harbor was loud with life. The hiss of steam, the clatter of hooves on cobbles, sailors calling to one another in a dozen different accents. Crates thudded onto wet stone. Gulls screamed overhead like warnings unheeded.

She descended the gangway with careful steps, the weight of the trunk following behind her on a hired porter's cart. Rain misted the brim of her hat and clung to her lashes.

Liverpool was gray and bustling, strange in its

energy—nothing like the England of her memories, which had been shaped more by bedtime stories than actual experience.

She spotted a bench near a stack of wooden barrels and gestured for the porter to leave the trunk at her feet. With a polite nod, she handed him a coin and lowered herself onto the damp wood, folding her hands in her lap.

And then—for the first time since receiving the letter—she sat still.

The sea behind her.

England before her.

And somewhere inland... a bookstore waiting.

She listened to the harbor.

To the sounds of men swearing and children laughing, to the bray of a donkey cart and the deep groan of shifting hulls. The air smelled of coal smoke and fish, oil and rope, old wood and new iron. Everything foreign. Everything familiar.

I shall stay the night in Liverpool, she thought. *Arrange for a train tomorrow. Then Haworth.*

The porter returned a moment later, breathless, to tell her a hotel coach was en route.

Primrose nodded, rising carefully and brushing a wrinkle from her skirt. She rested one hand on the trunk beside her, the other adjusting the satchel strap across her shoulder.

The harbor noise carried on around her, but she was no longer listening. Her gaze had drifted inland—toward streets she did not know. She watched as municipal buildings passed by the carriage window as they traveled along Victoria Street.

As they turned onto Charlotte Street she enjoyed seeing the various shops and the townspeople walking about. The driver maneuvered onto Ranelagh Place and came to a stop.

She exhaled slowly, the damp air curling past her lips. She looked out the window and saw Ranelagh Gardens and nearby, the Adelphi Hotel stood before her--a welcoming and grand building.

A porter followed her with her trunk in tow as she checked in and made her way to her accommodation. Inside there were elegant arches, fine furniture, imported rugs, and the superior craftsmanship of the architecture she could not help but admire. She heard music playing and as she turned a corner, she saw a small orchestra playing *Idyll,* a beautiful piece, she overheard a woman mention it was by composer Samuel Coleridge-Taylor.

She stopped for a moment to listen. Then she realized she was the only one—as she looked around her, everyone else walked passed—too busy, she supposed, to take it in. She couldn't help but feel the music was representing a new beginning.

Her room was quite nice, more luxury than she was accustomed to. A high ceiling with deep crown molding, a single bed in the center of the left wall and a window across from it. To the right of the window was built-in cabinetry and a washstand with a chair and mirror. The floor had a geometric pattern.

She asked the porter to leave the trunk by an armoire that was near the bed, and she thanked him as he left. She decided to give the bed a test and to her delight it was probably the most comfort she had ever felt.

Tomorrow, she thought. *Tomorrow, I begin.*

Her room overlooked the garden, and from its narrow window, she could still see the people going about their lives.

She unpacked only what she needed: a nightgown, her brush, and a small tin of lavender balm. The letter remained untouched in her satchel.

She arrived in the dining room just in time for the first dinner service. She had steak and kidney pudding and a gooseberry tart. Her eyes wandered the room of crisp white linens, on tables of two and four. The rich wood of the walls made the atmosphere warm, and the sounds of dishes and conversations made it feel inviting. She could distinctly smell rosemary but before she could ponder it her food arrived.

Back in her room the bed was firm, the linens cool and the city outside hummed quietly.

She fell asleep quicker than she expected—and dreamed.

She was small again.

The scent of old paper and candlewax filled the air, and she was standing in the back room of a bookshop—the shop. Her father sat in the circle of lamplight at a long worktable, his sleeves rolled, spectacles perched low on his nose.

He held something in his hand. Turning it carefully, reverently. A compass, gilded and jeweled, its needle trembling slightly under his fingers.

She took a step closer.

"It's lovely," she said, her child-voice clear and bright.

He looked up and smiled—softly, distantly. There was something in his eyes that she didn't recognize. Not sadness. Not fear. Something quieter. A kind of knowing.

Before he could speak, the lamplight flickered.

From beyond the shelves came a rustle of wings.

Then—CRASH.

Primrose was suddenly awakened by a rattle at the window. Wood and glass shaking. Feathers striking the pane.

She gasped and sat up.

The room was dark, the fog casting shadows through the thin curtains.

She pressed a hand to her chest, breath shallow. The sound had been real.

Cautiously, she rose from the bed, bare feet landing silently against the cold floor. She approached the window and, with deliberate care, pulled back the sheer curtain.

An owl sat on the narrow window box just beyond the glass. Large and unmoving, its mottled feathers blurred by mist, its round eyes glowing amber in the darkness.

It stared at her.

And she—frozen in place, heart slowly settling as she stared back.

For a moment, neither moved.

The hotel faded. The city, even the dream—gone. Only the owl remained, and the soft sound of her own breath.

Without knowing why, she reached out.

Her fingers touched the cold glass.

The owl gave a sudden, piercing screech—sharp and shivering—and then, without further sound, launched into the night, wings cutting silently through the air.

She stood there long after it had vanished, palm pressed against the glass.

"*I begin tomorrow,*" she whispered.

But it had already begun.

3 THE JOURNEY TO HAWORTH

The station was alive with motion, noise, and steam. She glanced at the Keighley & Worth Valley Railway ticket in her hand.

Porters shouted over the clatter of trunks. Children weaved between skirts and coat hems, chasing one another with sugar-sticky hands. Horses whinnied from the far end of the platform, where carriages dropped off their morning fares, and a great plume of smoke coiled into the gray sky from the engine's stack.

The air was thick with the scent of coal and wet leather, of fresh bread from a nearby vendor, and ink from the stacks of printed timetables clutched in travelers' gloved hands. The tiled floor beneath Primrose's boots was slick from the morning rain, muddied now by dozens of hurried footsteps.

She stood still at the center of it all, her gloved hands folded over the leather handle of her satchel. Her trunk had already been loaded by a porter into the baggage car, the latches secured with practiced clinks.

Her gaze swept the platform. At the iron girders overhead, black with soot and spiderwebs; at the elegant women in traveling coats and veiled hats; at a man near the edge of the platform whispering his goodbye into a woman's gloved palm.

Her heart beat evenly. But beneath the quiet thrum of excitement, there was sorrow—thin and persistent, like a distant bell she couldn't unhear.

I am returning to a place I no longer know, she thought. *And yet I feel as though something is waiting for me there.*

A porter touched his cap and gestured toward the nearest coach door. Primrose thanked him with a polite nod, lifted her skirt slightly, and stepped up the metal stair into the passenger car.

The interior smelled of wool and lemon polish.

The upholstery was deep green velvet, worn smooth in places, but clean. Small wood hooks lined the paneled walls above the windows, where gentlemen had hung their hats and walking sticks. Each compartment held two facing benches, cushioned and narrow, with small carved armrests and a folding table between.

Primrose chose a seat beside the window, brushing a few crumbs from the cushion before sitting. The glass was fogged slightly from the damp, and outside, she watched as the bustle of the platform continued without her.

A child waved at her from behind a pillar. She gave the faintest smile in return.

Then—

"All aboard!" came the conductor's voice, carrying over the hiss of steam.

The whistle blew, long and low.

The train shuddered once, then twice. A metallic groan rolled through the floorboards as the wheels began to turn, grinding against the track in a slow, determined rhythm.

And just like that, Liverpool began to slip away.

The compartment door slid open with a soft clack, and a woman entered—a few years older than Primrose, with pale blue eyes and a round traveling hat trimmed in gray velvet. She wore a simple navy skirt and held a book in one gloved hand, her other arm wrapped around a handbag that looked more decorative than practical.

She offered a polite nod before settling on the bench across from Primrose.

The train rocked gently as it gathered speed.

For a time, they sat in companionable silence, the sound of wheels on track rising and falling like breath beneath them.

Then the woman glanced up.

"I don't mean to intrude," she said gently, "but might I ask where you're headed?"

Primrose offered a courteous smile. "Haworth. West Yorkshire."

The woman's brow lifted faintly. "Oh." She hesitated, her tone softening. "You're brave to go alone. I mean no offense—it's just… well, I'd heard there was a murder there recently."

Primrose's gaze sharpened slightly. "A murder?"

The woman nodded. "A shop owner, I believe. Though I didn't catch all the details. It may have been months ago now. Still, such a quiet town. It stayed with me."

She looked out the window, her gloved hand absently tightening around the book in her lap.

"The world is changing," she murmured. "Even the countryside isn't what it was. Cities are full of smoke and strangers. And now the villages… well." She gave a sad smile. "I suppose nowhere is truly safe anymore."

Primrose tilted her head, politely reflective. "Danger, I've found, is rarely confined by geography."

The woman blinked at that—startled, perhaps, by the calm in her voice—but gave a respectful nod and turned her gaze to the window again.

So did Primrose.

The fields had begun to open, green and brown and gold beneath a soft drizzle. Stone walls divided pastures like patchwork seams. Sheep dotted the hills, and in the distance, the shadow of moorland rose against the horizon.

Primrose sat still, her gloved hands folded loosely in her lap.

Her reflection ghosted in the windowpane—serene, unreadable.

But behind her eyes, something had stirred.

The rhythm of the train lulled her into a daydream. For an instant, she saw not her own face in the glass but her mother's in the distance, in the fields—smiling, windblown dark hair undone as they picnicked in these same hills. She felt once again the warmth of her father's laughter rolling like the moorland breeze.

Her stomach tightened. That was the last perfect day.

Her breath came shallow, chest rising and falling as though she could not draw enough air. She pressed a hand to her bodice, forcing herself upright, fighting the pull of her memory.

Outside, the hills blurred. Rain traced slow lines down the glass. The family she had lost lingered there, just beyond reach—alive in her mind, dead in the world.

The countryside slipped past in softened hues— misty stone walls, hedgerows now blurred by rain, the faint silhouette of distant mills. The rhythm of the train became hypnotic: steel on steel, the occasional lurch around a bend, the low whistle echoing across the moors.

Primrose's lids grew heavy.

Across from her, the woman had returned to her book. The carriage was warm, the velvet seat familiar now beneath her.

She let her chin rest lightly against the high collar of her coat.

And sleep, sudden and full, found her.

She found herself walking through a shop.

Not the bustling stationers of her memories, nor the tidy storefronts of London—but her father's shop, as it had last stood in her childhood: dim, wooden, and full of shadowed corners. Dust drifted in golden shafts through stained-glass transoms. The smell of old paper and cedar filled the air.

Books lined up on the shelves in uneven rows. Some leaned together like conspirators. Others stood solitary and proud. There were clocks, too— mantelpieces and longcase, all ticking out of sync.

She moved through the aisles, fingertips trailing along the cracked spines, drawn toward the back of the shop.

There, beneath a green-shaded lamp, sat a worktable.

And on it, a single object.

A compass. The same one from her dream at sea. The jeweled face shimmered faintly, though no light touched it. The needle spun slowly—then stopped.

She reached out—Screeeeech!

The sound split the silence.

An owl, enormous and ghostly white, landed heavily atop a high shelf, wings outstretched. Its feathers ruffled like parchment in wind. It turned its head toward her—eyes piercing, unblinking.

Primrose gasped and took a step back.

Her foot struck something soft.

She looked down.

A single feather, long and white and edged in tawny, lay at her feet.

She bent to pick it up.

A sudden bump of the train jolted her upright.

Across from her, the other woman was still reading, unaware.

Primrose blinked, adjusting to the shifting light. The hills had grown steeper now, and the moorland pressed closer to the track. The sky had darkened—painted with watercolor clouds in varying shades of gray.

The whistle shrieked once, high and sharp, as the train pulled into the platform at Haworth Station.

The rain had stopped, but the cobblestones still glistened with raindrops. Smoke curled low from the engine's stack and the mist clung to the hills beyond. The hiss of steam and the clatter of boots on wood filled the air.

Primrose adjusted her satchel as she stepped down from the coach. A porter followed with her trunk, his breath clouding in the cool afternoon air.

She paused on the platform.

The Yorkshire countryside rose beyond the tracks—. it looked like something from a storybook. One she hadn't read in a very long time.

A man stepped forward from beneath the iron arch.

Tall and thin, with a dark coat buttoned to the throat and a bowler hat tucked under one arm, he approached with a gait both deliberate and stiff. His beard was neatly trimmed, flecked with silver, and his spectacles caught the weak sunlight as he inclined his head.

"Miss Eversley?" asked Mr. Withers peering over his horn-rimmed spectacles at her.

"Yes." She answered, feeling slightly embarrassed as if he was sizing her up.

"I am Mr. Ambrose Withers, solicitor to the late Mr. Alaric Eversley." His voice was precise, the vowels shaped by education and a trace of Northern edge. "May I extend my condolences and welcome you... home."

Primrose hesitated at the word.

Then nodded politely. "Thank you, Mr. Withers. It's been quite some time."

"Indeed." He studied her—not unkindly, but with the careful curiosity of a man accustomed to secrets. "The carriage is waiting. Your luggage will be seen to."

She glanced once at the hills, then turned to follow him.

As the porter loaded her trunk into a modest black carriage waiting beyond the station steps, Primrose climbed inside.

Mr. Withers joined her, and the door closed with a solid thud.

The driver gave a quiet flick of the reins, and the wheels began to turn.

Haworth, a town veiled in cloud and memory, awaited her arrival.

4 THE BOOKSHOP

The wheels clattered rhythmically over the stone road as the carriage wound its way through the village of Haworth.

Inside, the carriage was quiet, save for the soft creak of leather straps and the occasional rattle of the windowpane.

Primrose sat upright, gloved hands folded neatly in her lap.

Mr. Withers glanced at her over the rim of his spectacles. "You've not been back to Haworth since childhood, I presume?"

"No," she said. "Not since I was eight."

He nodded once. "Much has changed, and much hasn't. The shop is still standing, of course. Your father kept it in good order."

Primrose's brow furrowed slightly. "He was... well?"

Withers shifted slightly in his seat, the leather creaking beneath him. He tapped one gloved finger against his knee before speaking.

"In body, yes. In mind... perhaps less so. Toward the end, your father grew—withdrawn. Preoccupied."

Primrose kept her gaze on the misted glass, but her throat tightened. She traced the condensation with a gloved fingertip, a small spiral that broke as Withers went on.

"There were reports," he said carefully, "of odd visitors. Parcels arriving at strange hours. The sort of things that give neighbors something to whisper about."

Her hand pressed against the glass. "And his passing?"

Withers drew in a breath. His spectacles slid a fraction lower on his nose as though even they sagged under the weight of it. "He was found in the doorway of the shop one morning. By a neighbor." His voice dropped, low enough that she had to lean in to hear. "The door ajar. No sign of forced entry."

The village blurred beyond the window. Primrose's pulse thudded in her ears. "Go on."

"He had been shot." Withers hesitated, then corrected himself, softer. "Once in the chest. No witnesses. No arrests."

A sharp pang rose in her chest.

"The constable called it a robbery," Withers added, almost bitter. "But nothing of value was taken."

Primrose's breath quickened, though she forced her shoulders square. "So, it remains unsolved."

"Yes," he said. "Unsolved. And unsettling."

The carriage wheels struck a patch of wet stone, jolting them both. Withers steadied himself, then glanced at her, voice lower still.

"There are those who say he opened the door willingly. That he knew whomever it was."

Her fingers curled tightly around the satchel in her lap, leather creasing under her grip. She didn't look away from the fog.

"A murder there recently," the words surfaced like a pebble dropped into water. Not her own thoughts, but the voice of the woman from the train, soft and concerned, floating uninvited into her mind. *"A shop owner, I believe..."*

The echo curled through her chest, cold and unmistakable. Her breath quickened, just slightly, barely enough to be seen—but she felt it. A shift beneath the surface. A warning in her ribs.

The silence between them deepened, broken only by the sound of the wheels clattering over the wet stones of the lane.

Outside, the hills began to slope upward, and the chimney tops of Haworth appeared through the drifting fog.

The carriage slowed as they passed a worn wooden sign. The lettering, faded but elegant, read:

Welcome to Haworth. Est. 1209

"Let the moors keep their secrets."

Primrose tilted her head at the motto. Curious. Perhaps even prophetic.

The horse's hooves struck the cobblestones with a

steady, echoing rhythm—clop, clop, clop—as they entered the heart of the village. Fog curled along the edges of the buildings like smoke from an invisible hearth.

Haworth appeared caught in time. Perhaps that is what her father loved about it.

Old stone cottages stood shoulder to shoulder along the narrow lane, their shutters crooked, their chimneys breathing slow streams of smoke into the gray-colored sky. Gas lamps glowed with a soft golden hush at every corner, their glass panes fogged from the cold, their posts flaked with rust.

The townsfolk moved quietly in the mist—figures in flat caps and wool cloaks, wrapped in scarves, carrying baskets or parcels or lanterns.

As the carriage rounded the final curve and up the hill of Main Street, Mr. Withers leaned forward and gestured.

"There," he said, with something between reverence and caution. "Eversley Books and Curiosities."

The building stood proudly at the end of main street, nestled between two shuttered shops.

Its exterior was carved from pale stone, aged to a warm honeyed hue, with arched windows on either side of a brilliant blue-green door. The wood was painted freshly, the glass panels etched with delicate stained-glass flourishes in deep amber and sapphire tones that caught what little light filtered through the mist.

Above the door, hanging from an ornate wrought iron bracket, was a sign in curling script:

Eversley's Books & Curiosities

Inside, rows of books could be seen stacked neatly against dark wooden shelves, their spines dulled with age. Small curios gleamed faintly behind the glass windows—objects difficult to name, but impossible to ignore.

Flowerpots flanked the stone steps, each bursting with greenery and late-autumn blossoms—violet pansies, rosemary, and dusky geraniums. A single gas lamp hung just beside the door, casting a golden pool across the entryway.

The carriage came to a gentle stop.

Primrose stared up at the shop, her breath misting in the chill.

It was, unmistakably, her father's.

And it was waiting.

She stood before the door of her father's shop, the familiar blue-green paint now catching the golden flicker of the gas lamp beside it. The stained-glass windows, though darkened by the hour, still shimmered faintly with the last of the day's light. The smell of rosemary drifted up from a terracotta pot beside the steps, and it caught her off guard—sharp and nostalgic, stirring something deep in her chest.

Excitement. Sorrow. Dread.

She didn't quite breathe for a moment.

Mr. Withers joined her at the door, his coat buttoned high against the evening chill. "You've come a long way, Miss Eversley," he said, his voice gentler than before. "I do hope you'll find this place... welcoming, in time."

Primrose kept her eyes on the door. "This is where he died, isn't it?"

A pause.

"Yes," Withers said. "Just inside."

She swallowed, lips pressing into a pale line.

"I understand your concern," he added, more briskly now. "You needn't fear for your safety. The local constable is aware of your arrival and will patrol the lane twice daily, and more frequently if requested. The town knows you've come to settle the estate. There will be eyes on the shop—discreet ones."

Primrose nodded faintly, appreciating the reassurance.

"I'll send a carriage for you in the morning so we can finalize the estate paperwork," Withers continued. "But for tonight... this is yours."

He reached into his coat and produced a small silver ring holding several ornate keys. Each one was distinct—etched, aged, each lovely in its own right. He selected the largest—an old-fashioned skeleton key with a curved bow and worn grooves—and inserted it into the lock beneath the curved handles of the double door.

The latch clicked.

He opened the door slowly.

A warm draft of dust, wood, and faint citrus drifted out to greet them.

"Come," he said.

Primrose stepped forward, and he placed the ring of keys in her gloved hand. The weight of them surprised her. They felt important, like promises made in iron.

His man, a silent, serious fellow in a wool cap, began carrying her trunk and satchel inside, careful not to scuff the threshold.

Withers gestured toward the rear of the shop. "The living quarters are just above. Through here."

He led her past the first row of shelves, the glow from the gas lamp outside barely lighting their path. At the far end stood a narrow spiral staircase, its wooden railing curling upward into shadow.

He pointed to one of the smaller keys. "This one. It unlocks the flat at the top of the stairs. Your father kept it quite private. You'll find it comfortably furnished, though a bit dusty."

Primrose ran her thumb over the key's delicate design.

Withers looked at her carefully. "If you need anything, send word to my office. Or the vicarage—they'll see it reaches me."

She nodded, finally meeting his eyes.

"Thank you, Mr. Withers."

He inclined his head. "Until tomorrow, Miss Eversley."

Then he turned, stepped back out into the evening fog, and closed the door behind him.

Primrose was alone.

The keys jingled softly in her hand. She turned to the staircase—and the shadows above.

The soft click of the front door echoed like a whisper in the quiet shop.

Primrose stood for a moment in the dim light, the keys still warm in her hand. Then she turned back toward the entry and gently slid the bolt into place. The lock caught with a satisfying finality.

She slipped the ring of keys into her coat pocket.

The room was silent but not still. The kind of silence that breathed—slowly, thoughtfully.

She moved toward the front windows, the stained glass now reflecting only the gaslight outside and her own faint silhouette. Fog pressed up against the panes, blurring the outside world into shadow and glow.

Turning from the window, she let her gaze sweep across the shop.

Each step she took was light, deliberate, her boots nearly soundless on the worn wooden floor. She ran her fingers along the edge of a high bookshelf, its surface polished smooth by years of contact. A tall rolling ladder rested beside it, its wheels creaking slightly as she brushed past.

She passed a row of leather-bound rare editions; their cracked spines lined like soldiers in repose. One bore her father's old mark of cataloging—she recognized his slanted hand on a paper tag affixed to the spine.

Her fingertips grazed the spine of a volume on ancient cartography, then trailed along the glass lamp at the end of the row. Here the floorboards made a distinctive creaking noise. *Loose?* She made a mental note. *"Determine cause of the loose floorboard. Arrange repair—trustworthy carpenter required."*

Finally, she made her way to the front counter, where a tall cast-iron register sat dormant, its keys dulled by dust.

That's when she saw it.

Just beneath the counter's edge—half-hidden under the dark wood trim—a single feather.

She crouched carefully and reached for it.

It was white with tawny edges and when she lifted it to the light, it shimmered faintly, as though it didn't entirely belong to the world she knew. There was a faint coating of dust. It's been here a bit. She thought to herself. Odd.

She ran her fingers down its length—soft as silk, yet with a firm spine beneath.

"Gentle doesn't mean weak," she said, almost surprised by her own voice.

The duality struck her with strange clarity. The thought landed in her chest like truth.

She rose slowly, still holding the feather, and reached into her pocket for the keys. Turning the ring in her hand, she found the one Withers had indicated—the small, narrow one etched with a tiny floral pattern on its bow.

She looked up.

The spiral staircase loomed in the near-dark, its curve vanishing into shadow.

She took a few more steps forward, then paused.

"And just what have you left for me up there?" she

28

murmured to no one—and to him.

The shop didn't answer.

But the feather, gripped gently in her hand, suddenly felt heavier.

5 THE FLAT ABOVE

Primrose stood at the base of the staircase, keys in one hand, the feather still in the other.

In the dim light, she hadn't noticed its craftsmanship before. Now, with the shop silent and her senses attuned, she paused—and looked again.

The spiral staircase rose from the floor like something grown rather than built.

The railing curved upward in a perfect arc, smooth and seamless, without joints or nails. The wood was dark—nearly black—but shimmered faintly with streaks of deep red and gold when the light struck it. Not mahogany. Not walnut. Something older. Something unnamed.

She stepped closer, fingers brushing the baluster. It was warm to the touch—not in the way that wood retains heat, but in the way skin responds to another's presence. As though it recognized her. As though it had been waiting.

Her palm trailed along the rail as she ascended, the curved wood winding gently around a narrow central pillar that bore no sign of construction seams.

"How did they make this?" she wondered aloud. *"No joints... no cuts... not pieced together."*

She climbed slowly, each step careful, reverent. The air around the staircase was still, but not stale. There was a faint scent of pine resin and something cooler— like damp earth after rain.

Midway up, she stopped and looked down.

The steps wound behind her like the spiral of a shell, graceful and unbroken. The floor below seemed farther than it should have, as if the staircase had stretched, ever so slightly, in the act of climbing.

She laid her hand again on the railing, and this time

the sensation struck her more clearly—not just warmth, but energy. A quiet hum beneath her fingers. Subtle, but certain.

"Alive," she murmured.

Then she turned back toward the top.

The door to the flat waited in shadow, the floral-etched key still clutched in her palm.

At the top of the staircase, the narrow corridor stretched only a few steps ahead. It was lined in the same dark, polished wood—walls paneled with grain like flowing water. The corridor was quiet, except for the faint creak of her boots and the low sigh of air as she moved forward.

The door at the end stood solid and tall, its frame blending into the wood-paneled wall as though it had grown from it. It was made from the same mysterious timber as the staircase, heavy and ancient-feeling beneath her fingertips. No carvings. No handle—just a keyhole and the smooth, dense weight of time.

She slid the floral-etched key into the lock.

It turned without resistance.

There was a quiet click.

And the door opened.

Warm air spilled out, scented faintly with wax and tobacco and something floral she couldn't name—a scent she had not smelled in more than twenty years.

As she crossed the threshold, the room seemed to breathe. And then the sound came—light, high, uncontainable.

"Papa!" She froze. It was her own voice. The child she had been.

"My darling girl." His reply came with a rush of sound—pages turning, laughter, the scrape of a chair.

It pressed into her chest until her throat tightened, as if she had stepped through a doorway not into a room, but into the arms of memory itself.

She stood motionless just inside the doorway, her eyes damp but unblinking.

It was like stepping through a memory she didn't know she still carried.

She inched further into the room.

And gently—almost reverently—closed the door behind her. The latch clicked softly.

For a long moment, she did not move.

Her back pressed lightly against the wood, as if it

could hold her upright while the rest of her tried to remember how to breathe. The warmth of the room wrapped around her—not just in temperature, but in feeling. Like arms. Like an embrace.

She didn't want to disturb it.

Didn't want to let it go.

The echoes of laughter still rang in the silence, soft and fleeting. Her own childhood voice echoed faintly in her mind, too bright to be imagined, too familiar to ignore.

But then—something caught her eye.

Just above the writing desk, illuminated by the flickering glow of a nearby oil lamp, hung a framed photograph. Small. Faded with age.

Drawn to it like a moth to a flame, she pushed gently away from the door and walked forward, her footsteps silent against the worn rug beneath her boots.

She stood before it and stared.

A woman with dark eyes and a quiet smile looked out from the photograph, holding a bundled infant in her arms. The baby's cheek was pressed against her shoulder, its eyes closed in contentment.

"That's me," she thought. *"And her... my mother."*

Her throat tightened, and a slow ache bloomed in her chest and tears in her eyes.

And then—she heard it.

A whisper, low and close to her ear. Not imagined. Not internal.

"I loved her with everything in my being."

She turned sharply, heart thudding.

No one was there.

She searched the corners of the room, eyes sweeping over bookshelves, a threadbare armchair, a teacup resting on a side table, an old lyre dusty, half hidden in a corner—undisturbed, untouched.

The silence returned—but it wasn't hollow.

It shimmered, charged, like the moment between lightning and thunder.

Perhaps it was memory, she told herself. Or grief, playing tricks.

But something in the air pulsed—soft, warm, and familiar.

She turned her gaze back to the photograph.

And in that moment, it felt as if the room itself was holding the memory with her, not as a haunting... but as a kind of blessing.

Not to frighten her.

To let her know she wasn't alone.

Primrose drew in a steady breath.

And then another.

She lowered her hand from the photograph and turned from the wall, letting her eyes travel across the space for the first time with clarity—not as a grieving daughter, but as a woman with a list in her mind, as always, to keep the overwhelm at bay.

"Assess the living quarters. Take note of each room. Establish what is needed."

"Breathe."

She moved slowly through the flat, her boots whispering across the well-worn rug.

The sitting room, where she stood now, was modest in size but inviting. Gas sconces cast a warm golden light across the walls, and a small fireplace of carved stone anchored one corner of the room, filled with the faint scent of old ash and cedar. A plush armchair and a settee upholstered in green brocade faced each other at an angle, with a delicate inlaid side table between them. Scattered about the room were small, teetering stacks of books and newspapers, arranged with the kind of disarray that only came from constant use. Not messy—just alive.

"Living room: Neat. Warm. Needs dusting."

She moved to the nearest doorway and pushed it open.

The first bedroom greeted her with the familiar hush of unused space. It had once been hers—she could still feel the echo of childlike joy in the bones of the room. But her father had changed it. Now it served as an office, complete with a long oak desk, a drafting table angled toward the window, and shelves lining nearly every wall, many of them filled with maps, journals, and meticulously labeled boxes. A lamp still sat on the windowsill, beside a pressed botanical specimen under glass.

"Former bedroom: Now an office. Organized. Slightly cluttered."

And somehow—still hers.

She crossed the short hall to the second room.

Her father's bedroom was a study in quiet elegance. A tall four-poster bed draped with dark green velvet, flanked by matching mahogany nightstands. The wallpaper was a faded floral, likely unchanged for decades, and a tall wardrobe stood in one corner like a silent sentry. A small silver-handled brush and comb set rested neatly on top of a mirrored dresser, beside a bottle of cologne she remembered vaguely from childhood.

"Bedroom: Dignified. Still smells like him."

Finally, she entered the kitchen which was tucked behind a paneled door. It was small but smartly arranged, with narrow wooden counters, a cast iron stove, and a Belfast sink beneath a modest window that looked out over the back lane. The cupboards were painted cream, their knobs porcelain and slightly chipped. A set of blue-and-white china hung above the stove, along with dried herbs tied in bundles—rosemary, sage, and thyme.

"Kitchen: Functional. Charming. Nearly untouched."

She exhaled, longer this time, and tucked a loose curl behind her ear.

"Kitchen, water closet, two bedrooms, and one ghost." she said.

She didn't smile, but the thought steadied her.

The list was made. The worst was behind her.

At least... for now.

In the kitchen, she noticed a tin labeled Ceylon Tea on a shelf beside a crock of sugar and a small jar of honey. The sight felt like a comfort—tangible and ordinary.

"Tea. Yes. That, at least, I can manage." she said aloud.

She opened the stove's firebox, added a few bits of coal from the bin near the door, and struck a match. The flame caught, flickering to life beneath the iron grate. She placed the heavy copper kettle on the stovetop and adjusted the draft, listening to the soft tick of heat taking hold.

She left the kitchen and walked back into the office—her former bedroom, transformed.

Crossing to the desk, she sat in her father's chair for the first time. It creaked faintly beneath her weight, worn in places where his elbows must have rested, his hands must have passed over maps and ledgers and letters she hadn't yet found.

She placed the ring of keys and the owl's feather on

the desk.

It wasn't until the weight left her palm that she realized she'd been clutching them tightly the entire time.

Her hands ached faintly as they opened.

She leaned back in the chair, exhaling through her nose, her eyes tracing the contours of the room—the lamp, the bookcases, the panes of glass, still smudged with fingerprints. Everything here had known him more recently than she had.

Her gaze drifted back to the feather.

It sat slightly askew, pale against the dark wood.

Primrose picked it up once more, turning it slowly between her fingers. The light caught the edges, and it shimmered faintly

She watched it for a long while, saying nothing. Thinking nothing.

Finally, she set it gently back down on the desk.

And released a long, weary sigh.

Primrose rose from the chair, leaving the keys and feather behind for the first time, and walked quietly toward the kitchen.

The kettle trembled gently atop the cast iron stove, steam coiling upward in thin silver threads.

She reached for a tea cup from the wall rack—delicate, blue-and-white porcelain, with a tiny hairline crack along the saucer's edge. She recognized it from long ago, a set her father had always insisted was "for guests," though he'd used them himself often enough.

She filled the cup, the fragrance of the Ceylon tea rising to meet her—earthy and citrusy with a faint floral undertone, like orange blossoms after rain. The heat of the porcelain seeped into her hands, and for the first time since stepping foot in Haworth, she felt something close to steadiness.

She held the cup between both palms, not drinking yet. Just holding. Breathing.

The ritual had always calmed her.

Turning away from the stove, she walked slowly toward the bedroom.

The air in the hallway was cooler than the kitchen, and the shadows longer now.

She stood at the doorway of her father's room and paused.

She entered the bedroom with quiet steps, the warm

cup still tucked between her palms. The fire in the hearth had gone cold long ago, but the room held a residual warmth from earlier in the day, a faint scent of lavender and linen lingering in the air.

A small, upholstered chair invited her to sit near the window, its cushions worn but still comfortable, a knitted throw folded neatly over the back. Primrose lowered herself into it and sat with her tea, the soft clink of the cup against the saucer the only sound.

She sipped slowly.

The warmth of the liquid traveled through her chest, anchoring her.

Outside, fog drifted past the windowpanes, blurring the outline of the town's rooftops and chimney stacks. Somewhere below, a dog barked once, then fell silent. A cart rumbled distantly down a cobbled lane.

She stared out for a while, lost in thought, the tea cooling gradually in her cup. Her body was tired, and her mind finally slowed.

After a long pause, she looked toward the bed.

"You look quite comfortable," she said softly, her voice dry with sleep.

Setting her cup gently on the side table, she crossed the room.

The four-poster bed welcomed her without resistance. She removed her jacket and bodice—then eased herself down into the blankets, her hair tumbling across the pillow, her limbs grateful to be still.

Her eyes closed.

And almost before she could take another breath,

She was asleep.

6 MORNING LIGHT

Warmth touched her cheek.

Primrose stirred beneath the heavy quilt, the delicate weight of morning sun dancing across her skin in scattered, golden flecks. The light filtered through the lace curtains, softened by the sheer fabric and fog still lifting from the village beyond.

She blinked slowly, allowing herself to wake without rush.

And realized—

She felt rested.

Not just rested—restored. As though sleep had passed through her like a cleansing rain, washing away the heaviness she hadn't known she carried. Her limbs were loose and content, her breath deep and untroubled.

How odd, she thought. *I haven't slept like that in years.*

The bed, the house, the very walls around her seemed to exhale with her—as if this place had accepted her, welcomed her, held her.

She turned her face toward the window.

"Perhaps this is home. But at what cost?"

The thought rose uninvited, unforced, and hovered in her chest with an unfamiliar ease. Her life in New York—her flat, her library desk, her carefully built routines—floated through her mind for the briefest of moments, as though viewed from the far side of a dream.

And then drifted away.

She sat up slowly, brushing a strand of hair from her face.

Her gaze fell to her clothes—still wrinkled from the day before, her boots neatly set beside the bed.

"Well," she murmured to herself with faint amusement, *"that won't do."*

She rose and crossed the bedroom, slipping into the adjoining water closet—a modest but thoughtfully outfitted space. White tiles lined the floor, and a small wall-mounted boiler, likely coal-fed and recently used, clung above the basin with cast iron pipes exposed along the wall. A quiet tick and faint warmth radiated from its surface.

She turned the tap. The water, at first cool, quickly warmed—steam rising gently from the ceramic bowl.

It was a luxury for such a modest flat, and she made a mental note of it.

Her father must have had it installed in his later years—for comfort, perhaps, or necessity.

She washed slowly—cheeks, neck, wrists—the scent of lavender soap clinging to her skin, grounding her in the moment.

She dried her hands and stepped back into the bedroom, still warm from the sunlight spilling through the lace curtains. Her gaze drifted toward the bed she'd so easily surrendered to the night before— blankets rumpled, pillows softened by sleep—and then to the tall wardrobe in the corner.

A thought struck her. *"My belongings are downstairs."*

As she reached the bottom of the staircase, her eyes fell again on the trunk—still resting where the solicitor's man had left it the night before. It sat just inside the front door, squat and solid, its brass fittings dulled by travel.

She grasped the handle, gave it a testing tug, then paused.

The staircase, as graceful as it was, she had no chance of accommodating the weight of it—not without help.

She frowned slightly.

"Right. Adjust plan. Trunk stays below. Essentials come up."

She knelt beside it, brushing a bit of travel dust from the lid before unlatching the buckles and lifting the creaking lid. Inside, her familiar things greeted her like old friends: a few folded dresses, her worn but well-loved gloves, a small stack of letters tied with ribbon, and a soft shawl wrapped around her reading spectacles.

She began to sort through the contents with efficient hands, setting aside the garments she'd need immediately.

"Bring up only what's necessary for now. Wash dress. Air shawl. Keep nightgown within reach. Boots stay by the stairs."

As she worked, her mind clicked into its comfortable rhythm—order in the face of uncertainty.

As she reached for a silk blouse wrapped in brown paper, her hands paused mid-fold.

Her gaze drifted toward the windows, where the sun streamed through the stained glass and painted soft color on the floorboards.

"Am I really considering staying here?" she questioned herself.

She sat back on her heels, the silence wrapping around her like a question.

After a moment, she exhaled, almost a sigh, and murmured aloud:

"Well... I suppose that all depends on what these next few days reveal."

She smiled faintly at the thought.

Not quite a commitment.

But close enough.

Another note formed quietly behind it:

"Speak with Mr. Withers. Estate papers. Inquire about the shop's ledgers."

The list steadied her.

Primrose closed the trunk with a soft click and gathered the handful of items she'd chosen to bring up.

She paused at the base of the stairs, looking around the bookshop in the morning light—dusty, yes, but warm. Waiting.

It felt less like an arrival.

And more like a beginning.

By the time she finished bringing up her essentials and dressing properly for the day, the sun had risen fully. Soft light streamed through the high front windows, casting warm hues across the floor of the shop below. She descended the staircase once more, now in a crisp blouse and slate-gray skirt, her shawl draped over one arm, hair pinned neatly into place.

She crossed to the counter and glanced at the small

clock sitting beside the register.

Nearly half past nine.

"Mr. Withers had said morning. He would not be late." she thought.

Right on cue, the sound of carriage wheels crunching over cobblestone drifted in through the glass. A moment later, hooves struck the ground just outside the door, followed by the muffled call of a driver bringing the horse to a halt.

A dark phaeton carriage waited at the curb, polished to a shine despite the lingering fog, the solicitor's crest just visible on the side panel.

She reached for her gloves on the counter and drew them on, one finger at a time, watching as the driver climbed down.

"Time to learn what, exactly, he left behind."

With a steady breath and her chin slightly lifted, she crossed to the door and unlocked it.

The driver offered a polite nod as he helped her into the carriage. The seat was comfortably worn and within moments, the carriage began to move.

The iron-rimmed wheels clattered softly over the cobblestones, and Primrose enjoyed the openness of the carriage, the fresh air, the sunlight.

Haworth by daylight was something altogether different.

Gone was the dusky veil of fog and lantern glow. In its place stood a town of stone and slate, its buildings hewn from the same ancient earth that surrounded it. The streets, though narrow, were well-kept, with drains cut along the edges and gas lamps still flickering faintly in the brighter morning air.

They passed a row of small shops—each with painted signs, gold lettering faded with time but still proud.

They passed Fletcher's Butchery, where a young boy in a striped apron was sweeping the stoop, the scent of smoked meats drifting faintly from within. A striped awning fluttered above the door, and a chalkboard near the steps promised fresh sausages by midday.

Next came Hearth & Thread, a dressmaker's shop with bolts of fabric displayed in the front window— soft muslins, tartans, and dusky velvets. A small chalkboard propped beside the door read, "Lace trim arriving soon!" in careful, looping script.

Just beyond it sat Bramley's Tea & Dry Goods, its wide windows fogged with steam from within. The bell above the door gave a cheerful tinkle as a woman stepped out holding a neatly wrapped parcel against her apron, her cheeks flushed from the warmth inside.

They continued past a modest milliner's shop, where a fresh display of autumn hats rested on head-shaped forms in the glass. A bookseller's kiosk came next— tucked into a corner alcove with faded volumes stacked high in every direction. Then the tailor's storefront, with a waistcoat suspended proudly in the window, where two gentlemen stood chatting on the stoop, their voices low and companionable.

Children dashed across the lane, dodging handcarts. A woman with a wire basket full of bread loaves waved to someone unseen around the corner. Somewhere nearby, a coal delivery cart rumbled heavily, accompanied by the deep call of a man warning "Mind your feet!"

The scent of coal smoke, yeasty bread, damp wool, and horse sweat mingled in the air—a curious blend of life, labor, and routine.

Primrose sat quietly, watching it all unfold.

It had the slow rhythm of a place untouched by time. She hadn't remembered that about Haworth—not truly. As a child, it had felt larger, almost mystical. Now it felt contained. Rooted. Familiar in a way that was both comforting and disorienting.

They turned off the main thoroughfare and began to climb a gentle hill lined with hedgerows and narrow garden gates, the buildings now more spaced apart, stone homes with smoke curling from their chimneys. At the top of the lane, the carriage rolled to a stop.

The driver climbed down and offered his hand to assist her out of the carriage.

Primrose stepped down and took a deep breath.

As the driver tipped his cap and returned to his perch, Primrose remained standing at the gate, her gloved hands resting lightly on the iron latch.

The building before her was modest and tidy, two stories of pale stone softened by age, with ivy climbing lazily around the windows. A metal plaque beside the door caught the light:

Ambrose Withers, Solicitor.

She tilted her head slightly, brow furrowing in

thought.

"Curious," she mused. *"Why not keep an office in the center of town, among the bustle and business? Why here—up on this quiet hill, a step removed from the rhythm of the village?"*

It wasn't so far as to be isolated, but it was... deliberate.

Set apart.

She took one last glance over her shoulder at the winding lane and the rooftops below, then returned her attention to the door.

With a quiet breath, she lifted the latch and stepped forward.

"Ah! Miss Eversley," came a voice, warm and crisp with just a trace of Yorkshire in its edges.

"Mr. Withers" she said noticing his gray wool suit was impeccably pressed, though slightly dated.

"Good morning," she said, offering a polite nod.

He gave her a gentle smile.

He gestured toward the open doorway, stepping aside with a briskness.

"Come in, come in—we've much work to do."

She hesitated only a moment more, then stepped past him into the office.

The air inside was cooler than expected—still and thick with the scent of old books, leather chairs, lavender, and polished wood, overlaid faintly with something sharper—perhaps pipe tobacco. A clock ticked solemnly from the far wall, its sound steady, measured, like a metronome.

The walls were paneled in a warm walnut, aged to a deep amber sheen. Tall bookshelves lined nearly every surface, stacked not only with legal volumes bound in cracked leather, but also boxes labeled in tidy script— "Property Deeds," "Client Accounts," "Wills & Holdings." Near the corner sat a small filing cabinet, one drawer slightly ajar, its contents meticulously arranged with dividers and ribbon-tied folders.

The floorboards creaked faintly underfoot, polished but uneven from decades of wear. A wood fire smoldered in the hearth, its glow hidden behind a modest bronze screen. The heat didn't quite reach the center of the room, but it gave the space a lived-in feeling.

The furnishings were practical but handsome—a

mahogany desk strewn with correspondence, a green banker's lamp, a straight-backed chair opposite an armchair upholstered in burgundy velvet. A glass ink bottle glimmered beside a silver nib pen, and a single teacup sat forgotten on a stack of ledgers.

Mr. Withers moved past her and began shuffling papers on his desk with long-practiced precision.

But Primrose stood still for a moment longer, absorbing it all.

"This is where my father's affairs were handled. Where decisions were made. Where he came when he needed counsel." She thought.

She moved toward the chair Mr. Withers had gestured to and lowered herself into it, still looking quietly around the room.

"It smells like responsibility in here," she murmured.

Withers gave a dry chuckle. "Aromas of bureaucracy and pipe tobacco. Acquired taste."

He settled behind the desk and folded his hands atop a thick envelope bearing her name.

"Shall we begin?"

Mr. Withers opened the envelope with the precision of a man who had done so a thousand times before, but he handled its contents with care, as though the weight of them went beyond ink and parchment.

"You are," he began gently, "your father's sole heir, Miss Eversley. There were no other provisions, no trusts or shares divided. Everything—shop, stock, residence, and all remaining personal assets—shall pass to you."

Primrose's fingers curled lightly around the arms of the chair, her face unreadable.

Mr. Withers glanced up over his spectacles. "He was... quite clear about that."

She nodded once, absorbing the statement without ceremony.

"There's a formal reading, of course, and I will need your signature on several documents," he continued, shifting a stack of legal papers into a neat array. "But I should tell you—there is one item among his effects that bears special instruction."

He reached beneath the desk and retrieved a wooden box, about the length of a loaf of bread, covered in dark lacquered patterns, etched with symbols she did not immediately recognize. The corners were braced in gold, and the lock was oddly shaped, unlike any English hardware she had seen.

He placed it carefully between them on the desk.

"This," he said, "was delivered to my office nearly three years ago with a note in your father's hand. It stated it was not to be opened by anyone but you, and only after his death."

"There is also this letter" He placed it beside the box.

Primrose leaned forward slightly. The box gave off no sound, no scent—just an aura of distance, as though it had traveled far and waited patiently.

"There's no key?" she asked softly.

"With respect, no," Mr. Withers replied. "He did not provide one, nor any clue to its contents. I can only assume the key remains somewhere in his possessions—likely in the shop."

She studied the box.

It did not feel ominous, but it did feel... foreign. As though it held air from another part of the world. Another life.

She reached out and touched the lid with two fingers. The wood was warm to the touch.

"It's a mystery then," she glanced up with a grin.

Mr. Withers nodded solemnly. "That it is."

The next half hour passed in a blur of parchment, seals, and signatures. Mr. Withers guided her through each step with quiet efficiency, explaining the terms of ownership, property transfer, and residual accounts in calm, measured tones. Primrose listened carefully, asked questions when needed, and signed her name with a steady hand.

By the time the final paper was placed into its folder and the pen returned to its stand, the sun had climbed higher in the sky, casting long rectangles of gold across the carpet.

She glanced once more at the box, now nestled in a burlap wrap and tied with a cord for safekeeping.

Then she looked to Mr. Withers.

"Thank you," she said sincerely. "Not only for today—but for everything you did for my father. He trusted you."

The solicitor's eyes softened behind his spectacles.

"He was a difficult man to know," he admitted, "but fiercely loyal to those he loved. You, most of all. I believe this..." he gestured to the bundle "was not merely a legal matter for him. It was... personal."

Primrose gave a small nod, her expression unreadable but not cold.

She rose from the chair, and he did the same, escorting her once again to the door.

"If you should need anything else," he said, "my office is always open to you."

"Thank you again," she said.

He nodded once, solemn. "Safe journey back, Miss Eversley."

And with that, she stepped out into the sunlight.

7 THE LETTER

The soft creak of the floorboards echoed as Primrose crossed the threshold into the upstairs study. The afternoon light filtered through the curtains in narrow beams, glinting off the brass fittings of the desk and dancing across the wood grain.

She had returned straightaway from the solicitor's office, the wrapped box tucked beneath her arm. It now rested on her father's desk—silent, waiting.

Primrose did not sit in the high-backed desk chair this time. Instead, she chose the smaller armchair beside the hearth. She eased into it, the worn cushions molding to her.

From her satchel, she withdrew the envelope—her father's final letter.

It was heavier than it looked.

She turned it over slowly, her fingers tracing the edge of the paper as if reading the texture before the words.

He could have told me all this while he was alive.

But he hadn't. And that choice haunted the silence between them.

The seal, appearing as if it had been broken once and then carefully resealed, still bore the impression of the family signet—pressed faintly into the wax like a fading echo.

Primrose stared at the envelope in her hands for a long moment.

Was this what he could not say in life?

Would it explain his secrets—or deepen them?

Her fingers moved almost of their own accord, sliding beneath the flap with care.

The envelope opened with a soft whisper and inside was a folded sheet of parchment.

Her father's handwriting swept across the page in deep black strokes:

"My Darling Daughter,
If you are reading this, then I am no longer able to speak the words I should have said to you long ago. For that, I am sorry. The choices I made—particularly the one to stay in Haworth when you and your mother returned to the States—were not made lightly, though I know they caused pain.
The bookshop was never just a business—it was a threshold. Within its walls are objects that do not belong to any one country, faith, or time. They were gathered with care and kept with purpose. Many are harmless curiosities. Others are not."

Primrose paused, her hand shaking and her breath deepening.
She looked toward the desk where the box was still sitting, silent and sealed.

"I was part of something once—a circle of seekers, bound not by creed but by a shared hunger for knowledge. Some of us believed in preservation. Others... in control.
One day, they will come for me. They are not strangers to me. They are part of a dark faction.
There is a compass. You've seen it before, though you were too young to remember. It is not an ordinary instrument. It points not to north—but to truth, if you know how to use it.
There are others who would see such objects buried, destroyed, or worse—controlled. I have spent years keeping them from falling into the wrong hands. If you choose to open the shop again, you must do so carefully. Not all who browse the shelves come for books.
There is one man who may still be able to help you. Dr. Thaddeus Bellamy. An archaeologist of considerable intellect and unwavering loyalty. He and I have worked together for years—on digs, research, and preservation efforts far beyond what you'll find in any textbook.
If he still resides in Yorkshire, you'll find him near Settle. Seek him out, but do not do so openly. Use the

phrase: "We are all just fragments waiting to be unearthed." He will know it comes from me.

I pray you never need him. But if you do, trust him—as I did.

I left a second letter. I hid it where the light does not reach. You will know what that means when the time comes. You will understand.

I loved your mother with everything in me. And I loved you the moment I first held you. That has never changed.

Whatever path you choose next, do it with eyes open and heart steady. I do not ask you to continue my work. Only to be careful with what you inherit—and with who you trust.

Your adoring father."

Primrose's hand trembled as she lowered the letter to her lap.

She sat in silence for a long moment, the words circling in her mind like the hands of a clock returning to midnight.

She looked again at the locked box on the desk.

And then toward the shadowed shelves lining the sitting room.

"Where the light does not reach."

The story, it seemed, was only just beginning.

Primrose descended the spiral staircase slowly, the last words of her father's letter still circling in her mind.

"Not all who browse the shelves come for books."

She reached the bottom and paused, looking out across the shadowed aisles and scattered stacks. Sunlight filtered in through the front windows, illuminating dancing specks of dust in the air. It smelled of something earthy and arcane.

With a determined breath, she crossed the room and opened the curtains wider.

The shop came alive with light.

She spent the next hour straightening shelves, wiping away the fine layer of dust from the front counter, and setting the antique register right. A few titles caught her eye—volumes her father must've acquired recently. Others felt familiar from childhood, though time had worn their edges.

When she finished clearing a table near the front

window, she retrieved a small placard and wrote in bold, looping script:

"Assistant Wanted – Inquire Within"

She propped it on the sill just above a display of rare editions and stepped back to assess it.

"Might as well meet the townspeople." she thought, *"And perhaps someone knows more about my father."*

She made a mental note.

"Pay a visit to the constable."

She needed to know what they knew about her father's murder.

But right now, she needed help getting the shop ready for patrons. And with that thought, she clearly made up her mind.

Haworth and Eversley Books and Curiosities was now her home.

"Add another item to the list." she thought, *"Send a letter of resignation to Mrs. Hollingsworth, arrange for the shipping of my things."*

Her checklist was interrupted by the bell above the door which gave a soft jingle.

Primrose turned, smoothing her skirt instinctively.

A man stepped inside—tall, with sandy brown hair tucked under a worn newsboy cap. He wore a waistcoat over his shirtsleeves, a leather satchel slung over one shoulder and a notebook tucked beneath his arm. His eyes—blue and bright, with just a hint of mischief—met hers with a flicker of surprise.

"Ah," he said, "you must be Miss Eversley."

Primrose gave a measured nod. "And you are?"

"Rowan Ashcroft. The Yorkshire Post. Thought I'd stop by and offer my condolences... and perhaps an introduction." He held up the notebook slightly. "Your father was something of an enigma around here. Left more questions than answers, if you don't mind me saying."

Her posture stiffened slightly. "That seems to be the theme of the day."

Rowan smiled—not smug, but sharp. "May I?"

She hesitated, then gestured toward a chair near the window. "For a moment."

As he crossed the floor, she watched him carefully. He moved with ease—comfortable in quiet places, but not a stranger to secrets.

"He's charming," she thought, *"but far too curious."*

Primrose moved toward the armchair opposite Rowan and sat, smoothing her skirt across her knees with a practiced elegance.

"I hope I'm not intruding," he said. "It's just—I've lived here all my life, and I don't believe we've ever met. Folks were curious when word came that Alaric Eversley's daughter would inherit the shop. Most didn't even know he had one."

Primrose met his gaze evenly. "I lived in New York. I haven't been back to England since I was a child."

Rowan nodded slowly, as if processing more than just her words. "Must be quite a change. Coming from the city to... well, Haworth."

She offered the faintest smile. "I find the cobblestones and fog rather comforting."

That earned a small chuckle from him. "Fair enough."

He paused, letting the silence stretch just enough to feel deliberate. Then:

"May I ask—do you plan to stay? Reopen the shop?"

She studied him. His voice was casual, but there was something under it—a weight. A purpose.

"I'm considering it," she replied. "My father's affairs were more complicated than I'd expected. There's much to sort through."

Rowan tapped the side of his notebook absently. "Complicated how?"

Primrose tilted her head ever so slightly. "And are you asking as a curious villager, or as a journalist?"

His grin was immediate, a flash of teeth and confidence. "Can't I be both?"

"Perhaps," she said. "But I haven't decided yet which one I trust less."

That earned another laugh—this time a genuine one. "Fair play, Miss Eversley. I'll take that as my cue not to overstay my welcome."

He stood and tucked the notebook back under his arm.

"If you ever care for a quote," he added, "or just want to know which neighbors keep secrets behind flowerpots, I'm around."

Primrose stood as well, walking him to the door.

As he stepped out, he turned slightly. "For what it's worth—your father was a strange man. But not unkind. I hope you find what you're looking for."

She offered a polite nod. "Good day, Mr. Ashcroft."

The bell above the door jingled again as it closed behind him.

Primrose watched through the front window as he walked away—slowly, deliberately—not turning back once.

"Too smooth," she thought. *"Too observant."*

Her eyes lingered on his retreating form.

And then she looked back at the shop.

There was much to learn.

And not all of it would be in the pages of a book.

A flicker of movement in the corner of her eye drew her attention. Someone was hesitating just beyond the shop door—just a silhouette at first. Then, with a quick inhale, the figure pushed it open, setting off the bell once more.

Primrose turned.

A young woman stepped inside, clutching a worn leather satchel to her chest like a shield. She had chestnut hair pulled back in a messy knot, round spectacles that kept sliding down her nose, and a soft gray skirt that looked slightly too long for her frame. She wore a patched cardigan with a missing button, and shoes that had seen far too many Yorkshire winters.

"Um—hullo," she said, her voice barely louder than the bell. "I saw the sign... in the window."

Primrose blinked, momentarily disarmed.

The girl flushed. "The assistant one, I mean. I—I've read nearly everything in the Brontë Library twice over and I helped catalogue the new acquisitions at the Historical Society last spring, even though I'm not technically trained or anything, but I'm very organized and I—I don't talk much. Except right now. Obviously."

Primrose raised a hand gently, suppressing a smile. "It's quite all right. Come in."

The girl stepped farther inside, eyes wide as they flicked across the rows of books.

"What's your name?" asked Primrose.

"Margaret, uh Maggie. Maggie Thistle." The girl replied.

Primrose studied her for a moment. There was something endearing in her nervousness. Sincere. Earnest. A stark contrast to the smooth words and steady gaze of Mr. Ashcroft.

"And you'd like to work here?"

Maggie nodded rapidly. "I—I know I don't look like much. But I love books. And I'm good at finding things. I—I notice things. Details. Patterns."

Primrose glanced again at the help-wanted sign in the window, then back to Maggie.

She nodded once and removed the sign from the window. "Very well, Miss Thistle. Let's see if the shelves like you."

Maggie beamed.

And just like that, the bookshop no longer felt quite so empty.

8 LEDGERS AND LOOSE ENDS

Primrose went to the back of the shop and returned carrying three thick ledgers, placing them gently on the front counter with the weight of ritual. Maggie stood nearby, her hands neatly clasped, a mixture of excitement and nervous energy brightening her face.

Before opening the books, Primrose regarded her carefully.

"Before we begin, I want to set expectations," she said. "This is not a grand position, Miss Thistle. I can offer five shillings per week, tea in the mornings, and the comfort of a warm hearth if the chill sets in. If the shop prospers, your pay will reflect that."

Maggie blinked, visibly relieved. "Oh, that's more than fair, Miss Eversley. Truly."

Primrose nodded. "In return, I expect punctuality, quiet discretion, and an orderly mind. You'll assist with inventory, shelving, customer service, and organization. There are things in this shop—unusual things—and I expect you to mention anything that strikes you as... odd."

"Of course," Maggie said, eyes wide. "I—I'm very good with order and details. And I don't pry."

They shook hands across the counter. Maggie's grip was warm and soft.

Primrose turned to the first of the ledgers. "Now. My father kept meticulous records—or so I'd like to believe."

She opened the first ledger and pointed to the column of catalog numbers and titles. "This is the master catalog. Every book on our shelves should be listed here with a number. If it's not in the catalog, it doesn't belong."

She opened the second ledger. "This one lists all sold

items. If a book is missing from the shelf, and its number appears here, that is good."

"And if it's missing from both?" Maggie asked, her voice dropping instinctively.

"Then we make a note of it."

Maggie nodded, her gaze already darting between shelves and pages. "I can do that."

Primrose offered a tight smile. "Good. That will keep you occupied while I visit the constable."

Maggie's head snapped up. "Is it about your father?"

Primrose didn't answer immediately. She straightened the ledgers, then reached for her gloves. "It's time I began asking questions. Quietly."

She stepped to the door, paused, and looked back. "You'll be all right here?"

Maggie, already settling behind the counter with pencil in hand, nodded. "Quite. It's... peaceful in here."

Primrose slipped out the door and into the village the sun just falling on the horizon.

Maggie worked with a quiet diligence, checking the worn spines against the entries in the catalog. For the better part of an hour, nothing unusual caught her attention.

Until she reached the far wall beneath the rolling ladder.

A gap.

Two catalog numbers in a neat row—1247, 1248... and then 1250, then1253.

She flipped quickly through the ledger. 1249 wasn't marked sold. Wasn't marked at all.

She scribbled a note on her pad.

Then hesitated.

The shelf where 1249 should've been held only a single volume, shelved sideways—its spine blank, its cover old and smooth as bone.

Curious, Maggie reached for it.

But just as her fingers brushed the edge, the bell above the door rang again.

She jumped.

"Sorry—shop's not quite open yet!" she called.

A tall, older gentleman in a tweed coat and polished walking boots stepped inside with theatrical warmth, removing his cap as he entered. His mustache was carefully waxed, his cheeks red from the chill, and his eyes—though friendly—held a spark of something just a touch too rehearsed.

"Well, well!" he said, his voice a polished baritone. "You must be Miss Eversley. No mistaking the eyes— same thoughtful gaze as your father."

Maggie blinked. "Oh—actually, I'm not—"

"Of course, of course," he said, waving a gloved hand as if brushing away her modesty. "Alaric and I were great friends. He and I went way back. I was practically part of the furniture in this place once."

He strode farther inside without waiting for invitation, gazing fondly at the shelves as though expecting them to nod in agreement.

"Terrible business, his passing," he continued. "Terrible. But I'm glad to see the shop still has a pulse. He'd have wanted that."

Maggie cleared her throat softly. "I'm Maggie Thistle. Miss Eversley's assistant. She's out at the moment."

He stopped, mid-step, and looked her over again— this time with sharper assessment.

"Ah," he said, recovering quickly. "Well. Pleased to meet you, Miss Thistle. Perhaps you'll pass along my regards, then. Tell her... Harold Fenwick stopped by. An old friend of her father."

He smiled again, wide and practiced. "I'll come again soon. No doubt we'll see much of each other."

And with that, he nodded and turned, the bell chiming as he exited the shop.

Maggie stood behind the counter for several moments after Harold Fenwick left, heart thudding quietly in her chest. His words were pleasant enough, but something in his eyes—too smooth, too staged— unsettled her.

She crossed to the front door, turned the lock with a soft click.

At that same moment the bell over the constable's office gave a hollow chime as Primrose stepped inside.

The station was modest, more functional than formal, with scuffed wooden floors, a small waiting area and offices. An officer came out of the nearest office and said, "Can I help you miss?"

Primrose smiled and said I am looking for

information of a personal nature. I'm Primrose Eversley." He nodded and waved her to come into the office. A fire smoldered in the grate, though it did little to warm the air. The young man motioned to his superior while addressing him saying, "Eversley's daughter sir."

Behind a heavy desk sat a broad-shouldered man with a salt-and-pepper beard and sleeves rolled past his elbows. His eyes—gray, weathered, and lined from years of squinting at both crime scenes and gossip— lifted slowly to meet hers.

"Miss Eversley, Primrose is it?"

She nodded. "You heard I arrived then?"

"I've heard the whole village talk of little else." He gestured to the chair opposite his desk. "Constable Grant. Have a seat."

She did, removing her gloves but keeping her back straight.

"I'd like to speak to you about my father's death," she said. "What you know. What you don't. What was investigated. And what was—perhaps—intentionally ignored."

The constable studied her a moment. "Not one for pleasantries, are you?"

"I don't have the time for them." she said.

He nodded once, slowly, acknowledging the seriousness of her inquiry with the understanding that she means to investigate her father's death.

"Well then," he said, folding his hands. "Let's talk about the night your father died."

9 THE INVESTIGATION

The desk, broad and oak, was worn smooth at the edges and stacked with ledgers, ink pots, and blotting paper arranged in near military precision. Behind it stood a tall file cabinet, one drawer slightly ajar, and beside it a narrow coat rack with a dark coat and walking stick leaning against it. A kettle sat atop a small iron stove in the corner, its warmth barely touching the chill in the stone walls.

Constable Grant thumbed open a file. His gray beard was trimmed but not vainly so, and the watchfulness in his eyes suggested a man who missed little—even when he chose not to speak of it.

He studied her with a mixture of caution and curiosity.

"It's been just over a month," he said. "He was found early in the morning by Edith Crowley—the town historian. She came by to borrow a book."

He paused. "She found him just inside; the door was ajar."

Primrose asked, "Was anything taken?"

"Nothing obvious." Grant said, "That's the puzzle." He lifted a thin packet of papers from a file tied with dark red cord. "No register of theft. The till untouched."

Primrose watched him for a moment. "And Miss Crowley—what exactly did she report?"

Constable Grant referred to the folder slowly. "She gave a precise account. Too precise, maybe. But she's sharp. You'll find no one in town who knows the written past better."

"Or who guards it more jealously," Primrose said quietly.

He looked at her over the top of his spectacles.

"You've met her, then?"

"Not yet," she said. "But I know how historians think."

Primrose let the constable's last words settle like dust over the desk. Then she straightened, tone crisp but controlled.

"Was there any record of witnesses? Or anyone else seen near the shop that evening?"

Grant exhaled through his nose. "None that came forward. A few claimed they saw a figure near the square late—coat, hat, but nothing distinct. No one close enough to name. This is Haworth, Miss Eversley, not Whitechapel. We're not used to watching over our shoulders."

She tilted her head slightly. "Still, a man murdered in his own shop. Wouldn't that have warranted a wider inquiry?"

Just then she noticed a ring on his finger. Simple in form but heavy, masculine—silver, dulled with age and wear. Its face bore a curious engraving: a serpent coiled into a circle, but broken at the mouth, the head separated from its tail by the smallest sliver of space.

It wasn't a family crest or anything ornamental. It was older, more arcane—deliberate in its strangeness.

Primrose said nothing, but her gaze lingered a beat too long.

"Aye, we did what we could," he said, though not without a hint of weariness. "Whoever it was knew how to come and go like a shadow."

Grant caught her glance as he set the paper down. "Inherited," he said lightly, flexing his fingers. "From my grandfather."

She said, "It's quite unusual."

Before she could press further, he cleared his throat and rose from his chair.

"Well, I expect you've quite a bit to settle still," he said briskly. "Estate matters. Shop inventory. Town folk to reacquaint yourself with."

He moved toward the door, already holding it open for her.

"If anything new comes to light, I'll let you know."

Primrose rose slowly, surprised by the sudden dismissal. But she smoothed her skirts, lifted her chin, and crossed the threshold with grace.

"Thank you, Constable."

He gave a shallow nod. "Miss Eversley."

The door closed behind her with a quiet finality.

She paused for a moment looking back at the door. Then with a quiet determination she went looking for the local historian.

Primrose stepped out into the brisk air, her boots clicking softly on the uneven stones as she made her way down the narrow lane, the wind tugging gently at the hem of her coat.

"Where might you be hiding, Edith Crowley?" she murmured to herself, eyes scanning the clustered windows and quiet corners of the village. *"Surely not buried in the archives at this hour."*

Her thoughts were interrupted by a burst of unexpected color—tucked at the edge of the square, a flower stand spilled with late blooms in hues of gold, plum, and faded rose. Drawn by instinct and memory, she drifted toward it.

Michaelmas daisies nodded in the wind, their lavender petals trembling. Deep crimson chrysanthemums clustered beside orange marigolds, while dried sprigs of heather and berried branches framed the edges in rustic elegance.

The scent was faint but comforting—earthy, with a trace of something sweetly nostalgic.

Primrose ran her fingers gently over a stalk of anemone, then paused at a small bundle of rosehips tied with string.

"Planning a bouquet, miss?" asked the woman tending the stall—cheeks rosy, hands wrapped in fingerless gloves.

"Not today," Primrose replied with a faint smile. "Though I needed a moment with something living."

The woman nodded in understanding. "It's been a quiet season, all told—'cept for poor Mr. Eversley's passing."

Primrose glanced up. "Did you know him?"

"Oh, everyone knew of him. Quiet sort. Sharp. Edith Crowley always came sniffing round his shop, though. Like two crows picking over the same story."

Primrose's smile faded.

"Do you know where I might find her?"

The flower woman tilted her head thoughtfully. "Might try the reading rooms—she's fond of that old public desk by the church. Or the war records hall, if she's feeling pious."

"Thank you." Primrose said as she turned away, the chrysanthemums still bright in the corners of her eyes, and continued toward the churchyard with renewed purpose.

Primrose followed the curve of the lane past St Micheals, its stained-glass windows glowing with fractured light. Just beyond, tucked beneath the shadow of a climbing rose arbor near the reading room, sat a woman at a narrow outdoor desk—shoulders square, chin high, pen scratching across parchment with mechanical precision.

Stacks of ledgers flanked her like ancient battlements, and a dark cloche hat shaded her face as she worked.

Primrose approached slowly.

Before she could speak, the woman looked up—and froze.

Her eyes, sharp and flinty, widened with sudden recognition. The pen slipped from her fingers and landed silently atop the pages.

A whisper escaped her lips.

"Primrose..."

The name hung there, delicate as smoke.

Primrose blinked. "I'm sorry... do I know you?"

The woman stood, slowly, as if reeling from the weight of a memory.

Primrose searched her face.

"I'm Edith Crowley," the woman continued, adjusting her gloves with a quick, embarrassed motion. "Historian, archivist, and town pest, if you ask most folk. Your father and I... we were friends. And your mother too."

Primrose's brow furrowed. "You knew my mother?"

Edith's gaze softened, eyes misting again as though a veil of time had lifted.

"I did. Lovely and clever, with a voice like music when she laughed. She used to sing to you in the shop while your father worked at the counter. I remember it vividly." Her voice caught for a moment. "She was already planning to take you back to the States. Said she needed a fresh start—far from this village and its buried things."

Primrose felt her chest tighten. "She never spoke of that time."

Edith nodded slowly. "No, I imagine she wouldn't have. There were… complications. Silence between them, I mean. But they both adored you. That much was never in question."

A long pause stretched between them, filled with the quiet rustle of drying leaves overhead.

"I hadn't realized anyone remembered me," Primrose said finally.

Edith gave a short, wistful breath. "I remember everything, Miss Eversley. That's both the gift and the burden of my profession."

Primrose nodded slowly. "I've been told you found him."

The warmth in Edith's expression cooled. "Yes," she said quietly. "And I wish I hadn't."

A silence stretched, the breeze rustling pages and branches overhead.

Edith gathered herself and gestured toward the bench beside her desk. "I imagine you have questions."

"I do," Primrose said, stepping closer. "But I'll need answers that aren't filed away in your ledgers."

Edith's lips twitched into the faintest of smiles.

"Then you'd best sit down."

Edith's gaze drifted to the edge of her ledger, fingers fidgeting with the corner of a pressed page.

"I came to borrow a volume," she said quietly, "a rare folio your father had promised me—one of the older compilations on northern folklore."

Primrose's voice was calm but firm. "And when you arrived?"

"The shop was dark, but the front door was unlatched. I thought he must've stepped out briefly, though that was unlike him. I called out—once. Twice. No reply." Her hand trembled briefly before she tucked it into the crook of her elbow.

A tear left her eye as she quietly said, "He was lying in a pool of blood just inside the door."

She stopped herself, eyes darting toward the church's arched windows behind them.

"Go on," Primrose prompted gently.

Edith inhaled. "It's not something I'll speak of here."

Primrose frowned, glancing around. "We're in the churchyard."

"Precisely," Edith said, lowering her voice. "Even

sacred ground has ears, Primrose. And sanctity is no longer what it once was—not in this town."

Before Primrose could respond, Edith subtly pulled a folded scrap of parchment from beneath her ledger and slipped it into Primrose's gloved hand beneath the desk's edge.

"Meet me at the old windmill road tomorrow evening," she murmured. "Where the stone steps meet the ivy wall."

Primrose tucked the paper into her coat pocket without looking.

Edith resumed her writing, as if nothing had passed between them. "Tell no one."

Primrose stepped away from the reading room in silence, her boots tracing a slow path over the damp cobbles, the sky above now thick with clouds too pale to be threatening. The wind had shifted. Sharper now. As if the village itself were listening.

She walked with her hands in her coat pockets, fingers brushing the edge of Edith's folded note.

"Even sacred ground has ears." she pondered this as she walked back to the shop.

It repeated in her mind like a chime, muffled but insistent. There had been something in the woman's eyes—not just fear, but urgency. A message buried beneath the words she hadn't spoken.

The serpent ring. The constable's casual deflection.

And now Edith, giving her secrets folded on church paper like contraband.

She reached the familiar green door of Eversley Books & Curiosities just as the sun was setting. She was met not by the gentle jingle of the bell, but by resistance.

The door was locked.

She paused, brows drawing together.

Primrose reached into her coat and pulled out the ornate key. It turned smoothly in the lock, and the mechanism gave a soft click. She pushed the door open to find Maggie standing behind the counter, wide-eyed and pale.

"Maggie?" Primrose asked, stepping inside. "Why was the door locked?"

Maggie wrung her hands. "I... I'm sorry, Miss Primrose. After you left, someone came in."

Primrose's gaze sharpened. "Who?"

"An older gentleman. Said he knew your father. I—I didn't like the way he looked at things. Said his name was Harold."

Primrose felt a chill crawl up her spine.

"You did the right thing locking up," she said calmly. "Thank you."

Maggie nodded, but her expression didn't ease.

"There's something else," she said, voice lower now. "I finished checking the shelves against your father's catalog—twice."

Primrose stepped closer.

"Three books were missing. No record of sale. No misfiling."

"Which books?"

Maggie swallowed. "Two were written in Latin. Old. Hard to translate. But the third..." She reached below the counter and pulled out the book she found on the shelf—no title, and written in an unfamiliar language with scribbled notes. "It was handwritten. No author. No title."

Primrose reached for the book. Her fingers grazed the edge—and her heart stirred with something that felt like memory, though she couldn't say why.

She looked up.

"Leave your list with me, Maggie. And thank you again... for keeping things safe."

Primrose glanced toward the shop window, where the sky had begun to dim, a gauzy lavender folding over the rooftops. Lamps outside flickered to life, casting long, amber streaks across the shelves.

"You've done more than enough today, Maggie," she said gently, folding the list of missing books and slipping it into her coat. "You should go on home. I'll see you in the morning."

Maggie gave a quick nod, still visibly shaken but relieved. "Yes, Miss Primrose. Thank you. I—I'll be early. I promise."

"You're doing quite well," Primrose added with a soft smile. "Truly."

The girl gave a shy smile in return, gathered her shawl, and disappeared through the front door. Primrose waited, listening for the jingle of the bell and the soft click of the latch.

She crossed the shop in silence, locking the door behind Maggie. The heavy key turned with a deep metallic thunk. She checked it twice, then lowered the lamps one by one, their light fading into dim pools on the floorboards.

As the final shadows stretched across the shop, she stood for a moment behind the counter, her hand brushing once more over the uncatalogued book. She decided to take it upstairs.

She made her way up the spiral staircase, into the warmth of the apartment above.

She moved through the kitchen slowly, her motions precise but thoughtful—placing the kettle over the flame, gathering a few simple things from the larder. The scent of warm bread and dried herbs soon filled the room.

As she sliced into a wedge of cheese and stirred a pot of broth, her mind returned to the two missing books.

And the man named Harold.

And the mystery book Maggie found.

Downstairs, the shop creaked softly, as if the walls themselves were settling secrets for the night.

After supper, Primrose tidied the small kitchen and banked the flame beneath the kettle. The apartment was still—save for the occasional groan of the old floorboards beneath her steps.

She carried the mysterious book to the bedroom, placed it gently on top the quilt, and climbed in. The weight of the day pulled at her shoulders, but curiosity held her upright.

She opened the cover.

The pages were thick and brittle at the corners, filled with handwritten text in ink the color of dried violets. *"No author, no title"* she thought. Only symbols, diagrams, and lines of an unknown language interspersed with strange marginalia—some in her father's unmistakable hand but not all. *Whose writing is this?*

Primrose's eyes moved slowly over the page, a subtle chill creeping up her arms.

She turned another.

Then another.

Suddenly she saw that familiar serpent from the constable's ring. "Hmmm. Interesting..." she said to herself.

She got out of bed and went to retrieve the note from Ms. Crowly hoping it would be helpful. The note

simply read, "6:00 tomorrow evening. 1251 Umbra."
She sat on the bed still holding the note, deep in
thought. *"Umbra, I don't recall any street of that name
in town."*

Trying to recall her Latin studies she says out loud,
"Umbra is Latin—the missing books are in Latin, 1251
is missing. Umbra—Shadow."

She put the note in the book, laid down, and let the
book rest on her chest, her fingers still curled around
the edge of the binding. "What do you know of this
missing book Edith?" she said aloud. Her eyelids
drifted shut, and sleep claimed her gently, pulling her
into dreams shadowed with whispers and flickering
symbols she didn't yet understand.

The word Umbra pulsed once in her mind.

Then silence.

10 RIDDLES IN THE WALLS

The first light of dawn poured softly through the bedroom window, casting golden ribbons across the floorboards and catching the glint of metal wardrobe hinges. Primrose stirred beneath the coverlet, the scent of cooled broth and old paper lingering faintly in the air.

She sat up slowly, rubbing the sleep from her eyes. For a moment, she simply breathed, allowing herself to feel the stillness—the kind only found in very old homes, where morning light and memory seem to arrive hand in hand.

As she pushed back the blankets and swung her legs over the edge of the bed, her heel bumped something with a soft thud.

The book lay on the floor, splayed open where it had fallen. "Umbra" she said. "Shadow". *Could this be Umbra? I wonder what Crowly knows.*

Primrose leaned down to retrieve it—and paused.

Something white and creased was tucked loosely between the pages, slightly askew now from the fall. Not a bookmark. Not Edith's note. A letter.

Her fingers moved gently, reverently, as she pulled it free.

The envelope was unmarked save for a single symbol pressed into the wax seal. She knew the handwriting instantly.

Her father's.

Heart pounding, she broke the seal and unfolded the parchment.

Inside, Alaric's familiar hand greeted her once again—not formal like the first letter, but quick, precise, and intimate, as though he had written it in haste... or fear.

"My dearest Primrose,

If you are reading this, then fate has placed you within reach of answers I could not give in life. The riddles within Umbra are not idle musings—they are keys. Hidden truths. I've marked them subtly. You'll know them by their placement.

You must look to the shop. Not the shelves. The bones of the place. The frame. The stones.

Follow them carefully,
Your beloved father."

Primrose stared at the letter, pulse steady but loud in her ears.

She turned back to the book. The pages it had been hidden between were filled with riddles and strange sketches—archways, corner beams, ornamental carvings rendered with peculiar precision.

"I hold what waits but cannot wake,
My face is carved, my form opaque.
No key will turn, no clasp will slide,
Yet still I guard what's locked inside."

With Umbra in one hand, her father's second letter folded tightly in the other. She moved slowly, as though the very walls might respond if she walked softly enough.

Her voice, low and thoughtful, echoed faintly as she recited one of the riddles again and again:

"I hold what waits but cannot wake,
My face is carved, my form opaque.
No key will turn, no clasp will slide,
Yet still I guard what's locked inside."

She turned the words over like stones in a river.

She walked into her father's office and slowly scanned the room. And there it was.

Her steps slowed.

She stood staring at it—the box, carved with unfamiliar symbols, opaque with black color and heavy with silence. Her father had left no key. No instructions. Only that it was meant for her.

"No key will turn... no clasp will slide..." she whispered.

Primrose moved closer, sat down in her father's chair and pulled the box closer. Her fingers brushing lightly over its surface.

"My face is carved," she said wearily. *"My form opaque..."*

The final line fell from her lips like breath:

"Yet still I guard what's locked inside."

She stared.
It wasn't just a keepsake. It was the riddle.
She didn't yet know how to open it—but now she knew:
It was never meant to be forced.
It was meant to be understood.
She consulted the Umbra once more.

"Where the shadows fall but never shift,
beneath the step, behind the glyph.
Seek the curve that leads to flame,
and whisper soft the founder's name."

She read it again, then again—eyes narrowing.
"The founder's name? Alaric?"
"Beneath the step...the curve that leads to flame?
The stairs!" she said excitedly. With that she jumped up and rushed to the staircase.
"The step beneath my feet." she said as she made her first step.
The shop had always felt... alive. Now it seemed it might truly be speaking.
Primrose cradled the box in both arms as she slowly descended the spiral staircase looking for the next bread crumb. Its dark wood creaking beneath her careful steps and its manner of construction— extraordinary. She paused at the base, where the final stair met the floor—her father's words circling in her mind.

"Seek the curve that leads to flame..."

She glanced down. The last step was slightly off. Not obviously—but just enough that her fingers felt the faintest seam where it met the floor.

Setting the box aside, she knelt down and pressed her hands to the edge of the tread. It didn't give easily. She dug her fingertips into the narrow groove, bracing herself, and pulled.

The wood groaned in protest.

Dust sifted down.

And then, with one last heave, the stair lifted— revealing a hidden recess beneath.

Inside, carved directly into a piece of slate, was a glyph.

It wasn't a letter. It wasn't a symbol she recognized from any language. It was artful. Purposeful.

A spiral, fluid and elegant, coiled inward like a sleeping fern—its center flaring into the shape of a flame.

Primrose stared, breath held, heart pounding.

She reached out, fingers trembling slightly, and traced the spiral with her index finger. The groove was shallow, but still sharp after all these years. She could almost feel the heat radiating from that tiny stone flame.

Then, without knowing why—without hesitation— she leaned forward, closed her eyes, and whispered:

"Alaric."

The air shifted.

A subtle sound—not quite a chime, not quite a sigh— echoed from the box behind her.

She turned.

The box's lock clicked.

Primrose rose slowly, her knees unsteady as she turned her full attention to the box.

The lid had popped up, just slightly—no latch, no hinges, no sound of a mechanism. It had simply... yielded.

She lifted it open fully.

Inside, nestled on deep blue velvet, lay a key.

It wasn't like the others—the ornate brass of the apartment, the iron teeth of the shop locks. This one was slender, forged from some dark metal that shimmered slightly in the light. Ancient and unfamiliar in shape, with the head twisted into a spiral that mimicked the very glyph she had just traced.

She stared at it, drawn into its simplicity and elegance.

She took the key and twisted it into the recesses of the glyph until the flame lit up. She removed the key again.

And then—beneath her feet—a sound.

A low, grinding tremor.

She staggered back as the spiral staircase began to shudder. The wood groaned, not as if breaking—but as if waking.

The entire staircase twisted, slowly—descending into the floor like a corkscrew, its central column rotating as the steps folded down, sinking into stone.

Dust spiraled in its wake. Faint light spilled upward from below.

Where once there had been only stone—flat and solid—now there was an opening.

A hidden passage.

Primrose stood at the edge, heart pounding, the strange key clutched in her hand.

The unknown below beckoned.

And something—ancient, patient, waiting—seemed to stir.

Primrose stood for a long time at the threshold, staring into the shadows where the staircase had vanished into the earth. The dim light beyond was quiet now—expectant.

With the mysterious key gripped tightly in her hand, she whispered "Umbra" and stepped into the opening and began her descent.

Cool air rushed upward.

At the bottom, a long corridor opened before her— arched ceilings held aloft by support columns etched with glyphs similar to the one beneath the stair. Torches set into the walls grew brighter slowly as she passed, one by one, as though sensing her presence.

The passage led to a central chamber, wide and domed, with multiple doorways branching off like spokes on a wheel—each sealed, some with ancient locks, others with carvings she could not yet decipher.

Then she heard it.

A rustle.

Soft, deliberate. From behind the nearest door, its surface carved with a spiral flame—the same glyph.

Primrose's hand shook as she brought the key forward. She twisted it into the lock with a deep, satisfying click.

The door eased open with a low creak.

Inside was a small circular room—dim, but warm with the flicker of a solitary hanging lantern. Her eyes followed the walls from left to right. Stone benches lined the walls and one small widow near the roof let in a gentle breeze. At the far end stood an ornate perch, carved of dark wood and crowned in gold leaf.

Upon it sat an owl.

Its plumage was striking—white and tawny, mottled in pale amber and soft gray, just like the feathers she had found.

The owl turned its head, wide golden eyes fixing on hers.

It let out a single, piercing screech that echoed through the chamber and reverberated in her ribs.

Primrose didn't move at first.

Then, slowly, cautiously, she stepped closer.

The owl didn't flee.

It bobbed its head once, as if greeting her.

11 THE KEEPERS QUARTERS

Primrose could not tear her eyes away from the bird of prey.

The owl's plumage shimmered in the lantern light—each feather catching the glow as though dusted with gold. The steady amber eyes regarded her with an intensity that was both wild and knowing. For a moment, the underground chamber—the cold stone, the locked doors, the strange glyph beneath the staircase—ceased to matter. There was only the bird, perched regally upon the ornate stand as though she had been waiting all these years for this very moment.

Primrose drew a slow breath.

"You are extraordinary," she whispered, the words slipping out before she could think better of them.

"What is your name?" she asked. "And why were you hidden here? What secrets do you carry?"

The owl tilted her head, amber eyes fixed on Primrose with an intelligence that made her chest tighten.

A faint smile touched her lips. "You can't stay here, not when Maggie will be arriving soon," she murmured. "A glorious creature like you deserves better than damp stone and shadows."

Her new friend gave a low, throaty coo in reply, as though in agreement.

Primrose nodded softly, extending her hand toward the ornate perch. "Shall we go, then?"

The owl ruffled her feathers once, then settled more firmly onto the carved perch, as though she understood what was expected.

Primrose wrapped both hands around the base of the stand, surprised at its weight.

"Very well," she whispered, as she lifted the perch

from the stone floor. "Stay where you are, and I shall see you safely upstairs."

Primrose ascended, step by careful step, carrying both owl and stand. Once on the main floor, she set the perch beside the staircase. With deliberate calm, she placed her hand on the railing, reversed the sequence she had stumbled upon earlier, and watched in awe as the staircase slowly shifted upward, groaning like an ancient corkscrew returning to its rightful place. Within moments, the chambers below were sealed once more, leaving no trace of their existence.

She exhaled, her heart still quickened by the sight. Then she gathered the owl and the perch once more, climbing gently toward the living quarters above.

At the top of the stairs, Primrose paused in the entryway, her arms straining faintly beneath the weight of the stand. The morning light spilled in through the stained-glass windows, throwing patterns of color across the floorboards.

She shifted her grip, steadying the perch, and cast her gaze around the space.

"Well," she said softly, tilting her chin up to meet the owl's unblinking gaze. "Where would you prefer to stay, my mysterious friend?"

Primrose lingered in the entryway a moment longer. Some secrets, she knew, were meant to be kept—at least until their purpose revealed itself.

"You were hidden for a reason, weren't you? Bound by father's secrets it seems." She thought to herself as her chest tightened, though not with fear—with the solemnity of trust passed into her hands. *"Then hidden you shall remain."*

At that, the owl shifted, lifting her wings with a low rustle and with sudden grace, she took flight, sweeping from the perch and gliding through the doorway that led to the private quarters. Primrose's heart skipped, and her boots quickening after her.

Through the hall and into her father's study the owl led her, plumage catching stray beams of light, before she landed with calm finality upon her father's wingback chair. The same desk where Alaric Eversley had once poured over letters and maps, now claimed by his silent companion.

Primrose entered more slowly.

"So… this is where you wish to stay," she murmured.

She carried the ornate perch across the room and set it in a corner, turned slightly away from the window. Out of reach of prying eyes and shielded from any curious glance that might fall too long.

"There," she said softly, brushing her palms together as if sealing a pact. "Safe. As Father meant you to be."

The owl gave a soft, throaty coo—almost approving—she flew to the perch and settled in.

Primrose lingered by the desk, her body resting lightly on the edge as she studied the owl's steady, knowing gaze. For a moment, it felt as though the owl understood far more than she should—as though her silence carried answers that words could never hold.

Primrose drew in a quiet breath.

"We shall continue this conversation later," she said softly, almost conspiratorially. "Maggie will be here any moment, and there's work to do—so much work."

Her eyes flicked toward the shelves, for a moment, then back to the owl. But when she looked again, something on the shelf caught her eye—something out of place.

She moved closer and saw a rare edition of Wuthering Heights. Primrose's felt the heat of tears trying to break free.

Her hand rose, fingers hovering just shy of it—when a sudden knock echoed through the shop door below.

She froze.

Maggie.

Her pulse quickened.

The owl shifted, feathers whispering against her perch, golden eyes fixed on her.

Another knock sounded, sharper this time.

Primrose glanced once more at the book. She longed to reclaim it—but not now. Not with Maggie at the door. It would have to wait. She placed the spiral key on the shelf.

She straightened her skirt, and whispered, "Keep our secret safe."

Then, with one last look at the owl and the key on the shelf, she turned and hurried toward the stairs.

The knock came again just as Primrose reached the bottom of the stairs. She smoothed the front of her blouse, composed her features into a smile, and opened the shop door.

Maggie stood there, cheeks flushed from the brisk

morning air, her auburn hair tucked beneath a sensible cap. A canvas satchel sagged at her side, clearly heavy with whatever she had decided to cart along.

"Good morning, Miss Eversley!" she chirped.

Primrose laughed softly and stepped aside. "Primrose will do. Come in, Maggie."

Primrose smiled and caught the girl's gaze darting toward the upper shelves.

Maggie leaned closer, lowering her voice though the shop was empty. "You know, I kept thinking about the inventory. Those gaps. Books gone missing."

Primrose tilted her head. "Yes. I've been thinking about that too."

"They weren't ordinary books," Maggie said. "They were rare and the topics were...esoteric.

"You're certain?" Primrose asked gently, though she already knew this.

A silence lingered, heavy with unspoken questions.

Primrose folded her hands on the counter. "Then we must keep our eyes sharp. Missing books are one thing. Missing rare books are another entirely."

Primrose flipped open the ledger where Maggie's careful handwriting marked gaps in the catalog. She ran her fingertip down the column, lips moving almost imperceptibly as she read. Instinctively her mind arranged the names into her familiar, orderly fashion: *The Art of the Alchemist—Aurifex Manus. The Secret Commonwealth: Hidden Folk and Unseen Worlds— Robert Kirk.*

She thought to herself—*Not misplaced. Not sold. Hidden.*

The thought rose unbidden, sure as breath. Father had left these as signposts; she was certain of it.

She closed the ledger with deliberate care and met Maggie's expectant gaze. "You've done excellent work. Thank you."

Maggie flushed with quiet pride.

Primrose's eyes swept the dusty shelves.

"The shop needs refreshing before we can open it properly. Begin with the front room—dust, polish the glass, sweep the floor. Make it welcoming again. I must see to a few matters upstairs."

Maggie nodded briskly, already rolling up her sleeves. "Yes, Miss—Primrose."

As the girl busied herself fetching the feather duster

and broom, Primrose carried the ledger back toward the staircase, the names of the two missing volumes echoing in her mind like a whispered chant.

Alchemist. Commonwealth.

Clues, waiting to be found like Umbra.

Primrose stood once more in her father's study, the familiar hush of the room pressing close around her. She put the ledger on the desk and moved once again to the shelf and this time she did not hesitate.

Her fingers hovered for a moment before lifting it carefully from its resting place. The leather binding was worn but proud, the gilt letters along the spine dulled with age yet still resolute. She cradled it as though it might vanish. "Wuthering Heights" she whispered.

She looked around the room, but her gaze drifted inevitably toward the great walnut desk. She crossed the room, pulled out the chair, and sat down.

She opened the book carefully.

But then—her eyes narrowed.

A page had been dog-eared. Folded down with deliberate purpose.

She scoffed under her breath. "Father, honestly..." The archivist in her bristled at the sacrilege. Folding pages in any book was unforgivable—let alone one so rare.

And yet... her annoyance softened into curiosity.

If he had done this, it was not out of carelessness. It was a sign. A marker.

She smoothed her thumb over the creased corner, her heart thrumming with the realization that he had meant for her to find it.

Her fingers turned the folded page with care, the vellum whispering faintly as it gave way.

Before she could linger further, Maggie's voice rang from below, urgent but tinged with curiosity.

"Miss Eversley? You'll want to come down—there's a gentleman here asking for you."

Primrose startled, snapping the book gently closed.

"Later," she murmured under her breath to her new owl companion, who still watched her silently from the perch.

She put the book back on the shelf, sighed, and went back downstairs.

Rowan Ashcroft stood at the threshold, hat in hand,

eyes glinting with that practiced mix of charm and scrutiny.

As Primrose descended the stairs, she gently questioned, "Are you here to interview me Mr. Ashcroft?"

Maggie lingered by the counter, cheeks faintly pink. "You're acquainted then?" she whispered, and Primrose nodded.

Maggie nodded and retreated discreetly into the rows of shelves.

Primrose smoothed her skirt and began to blush. *"What's this giddy nonsense girl?"* She thought to herself.

There he was again—the journalist. Dark coat buttoned smartly, hair just a touch unruly from the morning breeze, eyes keen as ever.

"Miss Eversley," he greeted, his tone warm but edged with curiosity. "I trust you're settling into your new kingdom?"

Primrose arched a brow. "It's less a kingdom, Mr. Ashcroft, and more a labyrinth. One with dustier shelves than I'd like."

His grin widened. "Ah, but even labyrinths hold treasures. If one is clever enough to find them."

As they walked toward their familiar spot, he said with a slight bow. "I see the shop hasn't swallowed you whole just yet."

Primrose tilted her head, unimpressed. "Not for lack of trying."

His chuckle was low, easy. He took a seat by the window when she gestured.

"Sharp as ever." He mused, "Tell me—what is the greater puzzle? The bookshop or its mistress?"

Primrose took the opposite chair, folding her hands neatly. "You didn't come here to flirt with metaphors, Mr. Ashcroft. Speak plainly."

He regarded her with a look that lingered just long enough to unsettle—but not enough to rattle. "Your father's death has stirred certain... conversations. Ones some would prefer remain buried."

Her brow arched. "And you came to fan the flames?"

"To warn you," Rowan said softly. "And perhaps to see how much you've already uncovered."

Primrose's lips curved in a faint smile. "Then you'll be disappointed—I'm not in the habit of handing answers to men who fish for them."

He laughed under his breath, conceding the point with a tilt of his head. "Fair enough. I must tell you: there were men seen near the shop the night your father died. Not strangers. Men tied to Haworth. But their names..." His voice dipped lower, "...are dangerous to speak without proof."

Her heart knocked once against her ribs, but her voice stayed even. "So—a breadcrumb."

"A warning," he countered.

"A clue," she corrected.

Their gazes locked across the narrow space—hers sharp, his unreadable, neither willing to yield. And under the clash of wit, something else stirred: suspicion, danger... and a thread of attraction both recognized, yet neither dared to name.

Rowan's smile faltered just enough to betray the strain beneath it. His eyes lingered on hers—hazel, steady, unyielding—as if she might strip him down to his hidden depths without effort. He shifted slightly, forcing the smile back into place.

"I'd love you to consider me a friend, Miss Eversley," he said at last, voice warm but edged. "Everyone needs friends in Haworth."

Primrose inclined her head, the faintest of concessions. She let her guard ease—but only a fraction. Enough to release the tautness in her shoulders, enough to allow a breath she hadn't realized she'd been holding. The silence between them settled into something calmer, something almost companionable. For the first time, their conversation strayed from riddles and death. Books, weather, the oddities of the town—safe things, surface things.

But then Rowan slipped a silver watch from his waistcoat pocket and flicked it open with a practiced hand. "Alas. Deadlines wait for no man, and my editor is far less forgiving than you." He rose smoothly, hat in hand, and offered her the ghost of a bow. "Good day, Miss Eversley."

She stood but didn't answer, only followed him with her gaze as he moved to the door. The bell chimed softly when it closed behind him, the sound fading into the quiet of the shop.

Primrose lingered by the window, watching his pleasing build disappear down the cobbled street.

"A too-curious man," she sighed, "one who plays at charm while hiding far more than he reveals." She crossed her arms, grounding herself.

She would need to keep her wits sharp. And her eyes sharper still.

Rowan Ashcroft left Primrose's shop with his usual purposeful stride, but once the street bent away from her window, the rhythm of his pace changed—slower, heavier. The afternoon light slanted across the cobbles as he passed the newspaper office, the building that should have claimed his time and attention.

He didn't even glance toward its door.

Instead, he turned left into a narrow row where the town's neat storefronts gave way to older, darker facades. The air here smelled faintly of coal smoke and damp stone, quieter than the market square, the shuffle of boots echoing hollow against the walls.

He stopped before a heavy wooden door, its iron fittings blackened with age. He raised his hand and knocked once, twice.

A silence. Then a rasp of movement from within. A small metal slide scraped open at eye level, revealing a pair of sharp gray eyes that studied him in silence.

Rowan didn't flinch.

The eyes lingered another moment before the slide snapped shut. Bolts shifted. Locks turned. The weight of the door groaned as it creaked open on its hinges.

He stepped inside.

The air was close, thick with smoke from oil lamps and the faint tang of tobacco. The low-ceilinged room opened around a long table, crowded with men in dark coats, their faces half-lit, half-shadowed. Papers lay spread across the wood, along with decanters and empty glasses, maps and ledgers.

The murmuring stilled at Rowan's entrance.

He closed the door gently behind him, his features settling into a different shape—no longer the charming journalist with witty words for a young woman in a bookshop, but something sharper, heavier. A man among others, part of a gathering that felt more tribunal than meeting.

The seat waiting for him was at the far end of the

table.

Rowan crossed the room without hesitation; boots muted against the worn boards. The men's eyes tracked him—some curious, some wary, some unreadable. He slipped into his chair at the far end of the table, the scrape of wood against floor as he pulled out his chair was the only sound in the charged silence.

For a moment, he busied himself with the ritual of settling in—adjusting his coat, folding his hands atop the table. Only then did he raise his eyes.

Across from him sat a man leaning slightly in shadow, but the light of the lamp caught the hard lines of his face, the faint smirk at the corner of his mouth, and the cold stillness in his gaze.

Harold Fenwick.

The air in Rowan's chest tightened.

The table seemed smaller between them, the rest of the room fading into background murmur. The society's business would continue, the maps and ledgers discussed, the pledges reaffirmed—but Rowan knew that, for him, this meeting had become something else entirely.

The unspoken truth passed between them, silent and immovable.

And Rowan forced himself to breathe evenly, to remain the picture of composure.

For now.

12 WHAT LIES HIDDEN

Primrose bid Maggie a good night as she left the shop for the day. Primrose had a meeting to keep. *What would Edith Crowly have to say. What secrets will she reveal? And how does she know about Umbra?*

She went upstairs to her father's study. She remembered seeing a map of Keighly on his desk, perhaps she'd find one of Haworth there too.

As she sifted through the paperwork, she found what she was looking for. An old map of the town, but nothing called Umbra. *"Hmmm"* she thought as she noticed a small arrow scribbled in black ink. It was directly between the inn and the flower shop. She folded the map tightly and put it in her satchel. She decided to see what the arrow was pointing toward.

The door chime rang as Primrose left the bookstore; locking the door behind her before she went in search of this mysterious arrow. She wandered down Main Street in search of the flower shop. When she reached the flower shop, she noticed there was a small alleyway between the flower shop and the inn. She looked all around but there was no sign that read "Umbra" just an arrow worked into the cobbles on the ground pointing down toward the shadows of the alley. *"Well, there are shadows."* Primrose said to herself as she stepped into the alleyway and slowly walked toward them.

The alleyway seemed very long. Longer than any alleyway should be. When she reached the end, she noticed a small iron gate. Beyond the gate was a dirt path. She decided to go and see where this might lead. In the fading light she wished she had brought a lamp, but the moonlight would have to do. She could hear a small babbling brook in the distance, and she could feel oak leaves crunching under her boots. There was also a faint hint of Rosemary. *"That's interesting."* she thought to herself just then she heard some rustling in the trees. She looked up, startled, but then heard a gentle "meow". It was a cat.

"What are you doing way out here." she said to the little cat. The cat started to climb down from the branch to greet her when, suddenly, the cat froze wide-eyed, and with its hair standing on end, ran away. Primrose looked to her left to see what startled the cat and noticed Edith Crowley approaching.

"Primrose," she said, "I knew you'd understand my note."

"What is this place?" asked Primrose.

"This, my dear girl, is Umbra." she said. "And this letter is for you."

Primrose took the letter from Edith and glanced at it. She instantly recognized her father's writing.

"When did he give this to you?" she asked.

Edith smiled a sad smile and responded, "Your father didn't give it to me. Athena did."

"Who is Athena?" said Primrose, confused.

"Athena is your father's most loyal companion—his owl. Edith continued, "A beautiful beast he found injured right here years ago."

"The night your Father died, I heard a noise at my bedroom window. It was Athena and she had this letter in her beak. I knew something terrible must have happened for her to deliver this to me at that hour. I have not seen her since. I believe she is missing, or perhaps she just flew away. Animals can be persnickety." Edith grunted.

"If father was friends with this woman, why would Athena have hidden herself in that underground chamber?" Primrose thought quietly to herself. *"Its probably best to let her believe she has flown away-- that persnickety, beautiful girl."*

"I had found a couple of feathers in the bookshop but I haven't seen an owl anywhere." Primrose said nonchalantly as she placed the letter in her satchel.

"What can you tell me about Umbra?" she asked as she began looking around and wandering the area.

Edith took a seat on a large stone, one of a number of stones set in a semicircle that Primrose hadn't noticed before.

Edith began weaving a tale of such preposterousness that Primrose stopped and stared at her dumbfounded.

Primrose shook her head while Edith's words echoed as if in a chamber, bombarding her head and her heart. "Secret societies, dark arts, sacred artifacts?" Primrose asked skeptically. "You're talking about magic as if it exists."

Edith stood up with a smile and walked toward Primrose. She took Primrose's hands into her own gently and whispered, "It does."

Just then, they both heard approaching horses. Edith pulled the hood of her wool cape over her head and said, "Go back the way you came and don't let anyone see you."

Startled, Primrose hurried back to the alleyway, but not without turning back for a brief moment to observe from the shadows. A group was gathering and Edith appeared to be greeting them. *"Oh dear, father, what have you gotten yourself into?"* Primrose whispered to herself before running back toward the flower shop.

Primrose peeked around the corner, not a single villager remained on Main Street. She silently slipped out from the alleyway and made her way back to the bookshop.

Upstairs she greeted Athena, "Hello darling... Athena." She gave the owl a polite nod and Athena bobbed her head, amber eyes wide with acknowledgement.

"It seems you've delivered a letter for father." She showed Athena the letter in her hand.

"Thank you." She said as she took a seat by the window. Primrose opened the letter and read her father's last words while Athena watched over her.

"Primrose, my darling daughter.
I have in my possession an artifact that men would kill for and tonight they will come for me. I hope you remember the stories I've read to you and tales I've spun because you will need them now more than ever.
I fear that I have left you with both a moral dilemma and a terrible duty. I trust you will make the best of it. Be careful who you trust. Oh, how I love you, my sweet

girl. Remember…I have not broken your heart—you have broken it; and in breaking it, you have broken mine.
I love you,
Your father, Alaric."

Hot tears gently slid down her cheeks. *Composure now completely destroyed.* She thought to herself.

"I have not broken your heart—you have broken it; and in breaking it, you have broken mine." She said looking at Athena. Then gentle smile made its way to her lips. She knew exactly what he meant with those words.

Primrose stood at once and walked over to the bookshelf and tapped the spine of Wuthering Heights. "Clever" she said, "When I was a girl, this was my favorite story." She pulled it, once again, from its resting place and skimmed through it. Back to the dog-eared page.

She hesitated for just a moment before turning the page.

In the margin, her father's hand revealed itself—unmistakable, strong strokes softened by haste.

"Seek the truth, but tread lightly. Not all knowledge is meant to be claimed."

Primrose traced it with her gaze, a chill slowly running down her spine. Fragments of symbols drawn in with obscure references to other texts.

And below it, in smaller script, a final note:

"They are watching. Trust sparingly."

The words seemed to lift from the page, pressing against her chest with a weight heavier than the book itself.

Primrose closed her eyes briefly. Her father's warning was clear enough—and yet it only sharpened her need to know.

She looked again at the text, wondering what other secrets it might yet yield.

Her father's hand had sketched a sigil in the corner—unsteady in ink, yet deliberate in form. At first glance it seemed abstract, but the longer she looked, the more the design revealed itself.

A pyramid formed the base, its lines sharp and unyielding. Within it, inked in dense strokes, burned a small flame—contained, protected, yet restless.

But it was what rose from that flame that unsettled her most: a spiral, but not of lines alone. The spiral itself shaped the body of a dragon, coiled tightly in upon itself, its head emerging at the center of the fire. Its eyes, drawn with two deft marks of her father's pen, seemed to watch her even now.

A flame within a pyramid.

A dragon hidden within a spiral.

Power bound and secreted away.

Beneath it, in her father's unmistakable hand, a single warning:

"What is caged burns brighter."

Primrose leaned closer, eyes tracing the sharp angles of the pyramid and the coiling dragon twisting through flame. The words echoed in her mind: *"They are watching. Trust sparingly."*

"Father... what had you entangled yourself in?" she whispered.

Suddenly something caught her eye. "What is that?" she whispered.

"Is that a tiny door?"

Hidden in the shelf's shadow, was the compartment her father had fashioned himself. It was a throwback to his carpentry hobby she remembered it now. "You see it, Prim? The wood grain tricks your eyes." She pressed on a thin line, and the trap door gave way on its hidden hinge.

13 THE COMPASS OF SECRETS

Primrose sat in her father's study, the jeweled compass resting delicately on her palm.

It gleamed in the firelight, its gold filigree and inlaid stones shimmering faintly. The needle quivered, but it did not settle on north. It did not settle at all.

Instead, it jerked in tiny motions, as if resisting some unseen pull, then swung decisively—not toward a direction of the earth, but toward the bookshelf across the room.

She turned it slowly in her hands, expecting the needle to swing back. It did not. It tugged again toward the shelf, insistent.

Athena let out a low, deliberate hoot, her golden eyes fixed in the same direction.

Primrose's heart gave a jolt. *"You see it too, don't you?"*

The owl did not move, but her unblinking gaze was answer enough.

Primrose shifted the compass. Again, it refused to orient itself as any natural compass would. Desk, shelf, drawer—the needle aligned only to objects in the study, as though magnetized to secrets rather than the earth.

Primrose stood up from the desk, the compass steady in her hand. The needle quivered, pulling her toward the tall bookshelf against the wall.

Her father's cataloguing had always been impeccable—rows aligned, spines neat, titles ordered as if each volume had been placed by rule and measure. But as her gaze traveled along the shelves, one spine disrupted the perfection. She laid the compass on a lower shelf, then she studied the book and gently pulled it.

A book of maps. Its faded leather cover bore the same sigil she had seen the day before, inlaid but with the gold nearly worn away with use.

Primrose's heart beat faster. This was not one of the missing texts Maggie had listed. Which meant it was something else—something her father had wanted her to find.

She reached out and ran her finger along the edge. The book was heavier than she expected, the leather cool beneath her touch.

Behind her, Athena gave a low, throaty coo, wings rustling.

She looked at Athena and asked her, *"Do you know what is in here?"*

The owl tilted her head, golden eyes unblinking, as though the question were not rhetorical at all.

Primrose pressed the book against her chest for a heartbeat, anticipation crackling through her like static. Then, unable to resist, she hurried back to the desk, set it down, and eased open the cover.

The first few pages were filled with exquisite, hand-drawn maps—vellum browned with age, the ink fine yet vivid. She lingered over one of Egypt, the pyramids rendered with startling precision, annotated in the margins with neat Latin script. Another showed Persia, where faint notations—arrows, circles, and symbols resembling the glyph she had seen—hinted at connections to the compass itself.

These were not simple reference maps; they were research, deliberate and personal.

As she turned another page, something slipped and crinkled. Between the leaves was a folded scrap, heavier paper, tucked in almost carelessly. She drew it free.

It was a another map of Haworth. Only this map looked much older, archaic.

The familiar outline of the moors and some of the streets spread before her in her father's hand. Notes crowded the margins: arrows pointing to alleys, cryptic words underlined twice, symbols that echoed those she had begun to piece together. He had been searching for something—here in Haworth—something hidden in plain sight.

Her pulse quickened. She smoothed the map flat on the desk, eyes darting over every detail. The shop was marked. So too were a few outlying cottages. And near the edge of town, just where the moor began to darken into wilderness, her father had drawn a spiral.

Primrose leaned back, pressing a hand over her lips.

"I'll need to wait until well past dusk," she whispered, the thought crystallizing even as she spoke it. "When the town sleeps, I'll see what Father left for me to find."

Behind her, Athena shifted on her perch, feathers whispering in the silence, as though the owl already knew what the night would bring.

As the hours passed, she sat at her father's desk, looking at the map with anticipation, but her stomach gave a small growl that reminded her she had neglected supper. She glanced at Athena, who ruffled her feathers as if in agreement.

"Well then," Primrose said softly, "shall we see what the kitchen holds for us?"

The owl gave a low, approving coo, hopping once on her perch.

In the small kitchen, Primrose lit a lamp and stirred the embers in the stove back to life. She found a portion of raw meat left from the butcher's parcel and placed it in a shallow dish. Setting it on the table, she inclined her head toward Athena. "For you, darling. I hope it suits."

Athena stepped down with a graceful beat of wings, talons clicking against the wood. She bent to the dish with a satisfied rustle, feathers shivering in delight.

Primrose, meanwhile, gathered onions, carrots, and a bit of mutton into a pot. As the stew began to simmer, filling the room with the familiar comfort of herbs and broth, she sat opposite the owl, chin resting lightly in her hand.

"You and I make a peculiar household," she mused, watching the flame's glow play across Athena's plumage. "But perhaps we'll manage."

Athena paused long enough to fix her amber eyes on Primrose—steady, unblinking, strangely reassuring— before returning to her meal.

Primrose smiled faintly, turning back to stir the stew.

The hour was edging toward midnight when Primrose returned to her father's study. The fire had burned down to embers, casting the room in a copper glow. She spread the map across the desk one last time, tracing the careful lines of her father's hand with her fingertip. Haworth—her Haworth—yet marked with curious notations, as though her father had been searching for something hidden beneath its cobbled streets and moors.

She folded the parchment neatly and slipped it into her coat pocket, her heart beating a fraction quicker.

Turning to Athena, she whispered, "We can't risk anyone seeing you. Go on, love—wait for me in the square. I'll find you there."

The owl tilted her head, feathers rippling in the lamplight. Primrose unlatched the window, and Athena swept out into the cool night, vanishing toward the heart of the town.

Primrose paused for a moment, for any sounds, but all was silent. Then she extinguished the lamp, smoothed her skirts, and slipped quietly downstairs. The shop lay still, shadows pooling between the shelves. She drew the bolt back carefully and stepped into the night air.

The waxing moon hung high, pale silver washing over rooftops and narrow lanes. She kept to the edges of the street, her boots soft against the stones. No lantern was needed; the moonlight offered just enough to move unseen.

Ahead, in the small square at the center of Haworth, Athena waited in the branches of a great elm, her tawny plumage melting into the shadows, her amber eyes gleaming like embers in the dark.

Primrose drew in a steadying breath. The town slept around her, unaware. Tonight, she would walk its hidden paths, and perhaps... find what her father had been searching for.

Primrose paused beneath the elm and drew the folded map from her pocket. She spread it open carefully, the moonlight glancing off the inked lines of Haworth her father had drawn by hand.

She lifted her eyes to Athena. *"Where shall we begin?"*

The owl gave a soft, throaty sound and shifted on her branch, amber gaze fixed intently on the page. Almost impossibly, as if compelled, the jeweled compass in Primrose's hand tilted toward a corner of the map.

Primrose followed its line and looked back to Athena. *"Here?"* she asked.

The owl spread her wings and swept into the air, gliding toward the indicated street.

Heart racing, Primrose gathered her courage and hurried after her. Each time Athena vanished over the rooftops, she reappeared on a new perch—waiting, watching, urging her forward. The compass needle quivered in alignment, and the map seemed to steady her hand, showing each narrow passage and lane as though her father himself were leading her through the night.

Athena's pale form swept ahead, wings ghosting over rooftops until she alighted on the dark stone ledge of St. Michael's Church.

Primrose slowed as she approached, breath misting in the cool night air. The jeweled compass quivered, its needle pointing steadily toward the church doors.

Athena gave a low, deliberate hoot and shifted along the carved masonry, her talons scraping lightly until she stalled before a section of ornamentation.

At first glance, it seemed nothing more than a flourish in the church's gothic design—interlacing vines and curling stonework. But as Primrose stepped closer, holding the map against the moonlight, her eyes caught the unmistakable pattern hidden within the artistry: a pyramid, its lines subtle but undeniable, spiraled through by the body of a dragon. Within its center, a small flame had been etched so delicately it might have been mistaken for shadow.

Her stomach tightened. It was the same sigil her father had drawn.

She reached up, brushing her gloved fingertips along the cold stone, feeling the grooves as if to confirm it was truly there.

"Athena..." Her voice was little more than a whisper. "How many have walked past this without ever seeing?"

The owl blinked, slow and deliberate, as if she alone knew the answer.

Athena shifted suddenly, her head swiveling all the way back, then snapping forward toward Primrose with a sharp, piercing gaze.

Before Primrose could react, the owl launched into silent flight. Wings swept the air with a single powerful beat, and in a flash of talons Athena snatched the compass cleanly from her hand.

"Athena!" Primrose hissed under her breath, but the owl was already gone—vanishing into the shadows of a nearby yew, the jeweled instrument glinting once before darkness swallowed it whole.

Primrose froze, heart thundering. She didn't need to hear it to know—footsteps. Steady, approaching. The air itself seemed to tighten around her.

Without thinking, she folded the map swiftly and tucked it deep into her jacket pocket, her fingers trembling against the stiff paper. Her breath came quick, chest rising and falling as she forced herself into stillness, waiting.

The steps rounded the corner.

And there he was.

Rowan Ashcroft.

His face emerged from the dim, caught half in shadow, half in moonlight. Familiar. Too familiar.

"Miss Eversley," he said, caught off guard—his eyes searched hers with unsettling sharpness, but the flicker of guilt was unmistakable. For just an instant, it was as if she'd stumbled upon him in the middle of something he hadn't meant her to see.

"You startled me," Primrose said, pulse quickening though her tone was steady.

Rowan arched a brow, still recovering from the surprise. "What are you doing here, Primrose?"

Is he scolding me? She crossed her arms lightly, tilting her chin. "I might ask you the same. It isn't often one finds a newspaperman lurking by a church at this hour."

He managed a thin smile. "Following a lead for a story."

Primrose's lips curved, though her eyes did not soften. "And I... could not sleep. I remembered seeing valerian in the churchyard when I passed earlier. Thought I might gather some for tea. It's said to quiet the nerves."

Her words hung between them—plausible enough, yet Rowan's searching gaze suggested he weighed every syllable for what she hadn't said.

Rowan's eyes darted left, then right, scanning the shadows that clung to the church walls. His unease set Primrose on edge—if a man like Rowan Ashcroft appeared nervous, then perhaps there truly were others lurking in the dark.

Without another word, he stepped closer and bent to the patch of valerian, plucking a stem with practiced ease.

"Here," he said, handing it to her, his voice quieter now, more measured. "You shouldn't be kneeling in the dirt at this hour."

Primrose accepted the herb, though her thoughts raced. Why was he here—really? She bent to gather another sprig, her gloves brushing damp leaves, and felt his presence at her side, steady and close. Together they collected a modest handful, though the silence between them was louder than any words.

When at last he straightened, Rowan glanced toward the narrow lane.

"Allow me to walk you back," he said firmly, leaving no room for argument.

She hesitated only a breath before nodding. The streets were hushed, the town sleeping under the waxing moon. Athena ghosted above them, wings silent as smoke, her pale form a fleeting shadow from rooftop to tree. She followed at a careful distance, keeping herself hidden from Rowan's eyes.

They reached the bookshop in silence, lantern-light flickering faintly from within. Rowan turned toward her as she placed her hand on the latch. For a heartbeat, neither spoke.

Then, unexpectedly, his fingers closed gently around her arm. He leaned closer, his breath warm against her ear, his voice low and taut with something between warning and concern.

"Please," he said, the word almost a plea. "Do not wander the streets at night. It isn't safe."

Before she could reply, he released her, tipping his hat with a guarded half-smile before stepping back into the night.

Primrose watched him go, her pulse still quick, knowing the danger was not only in the shadows but in what he stirred within her.

Inside, Primrose turned the key firmly in the lock, her hand lingering on the cool metal as if to steady herself. The hush of the shop pressed close around her.

Above, a faint rustle—soft, deliberate—broke the silence. Athena.

Relief bloomed through her chest. She hurried up the stairs, the creak of each step swallowed by her quickening breath.

In the study, Athena awaited her, feathers catching the moonlight that spilled through the tall window. The owl's amber eyes fixed on her with a knowing depth, and Primrose's tension eased as she crossed the room.

"There you are," she whispered. She lifted a hand to caress her, and Athena dipped her head, solemn and steady, as though she too had been guarding secrets in the night.

Athena leaned forward, releasing the jeweled compass into her palm with a deliberate snap of her talons before hopping back to her perch.

Primrose closed the window against the chill and turned back to the room. She placed the compass back in its hiding place, then withdrew the folded map from her pocket. The paper crackled softly as she smoothed it across the wood.

Pacing the room, she thought out loud.

"The church," she said. *"What secrets are carved into its stones?"*

Athena gave a low, throaty sound in response, as if urging her onward.

"Tomorrow," she told Athena firmly. *"At first light, I'll return and see what I will find."*

Athena blinked slowly, her amber eyes never leaving Primrose's face, as though she understood every word.

Morning light slanted through the bookshop's wide front windows, casting warm gold across the little table where Primrose had set out two cups of tea. Steam curled upward, carrying the soft scent of bergamot.

Maggie sat opposite her, a little out of breath from sweeping, her cheeks flushed pink. She wrapped her hands around the porcelain as though for comfort.

"It's kind of you, miss," she said shyly, lifting the cup. "Not everyone takes tea with the help."

Primrose gave a soft laugh. "Then they've no sense at all. You're not just 'the help,' Maggie. You've already done more to set this shop to rights than I could have alone."

Maggie's lips curved into a tentative smile, but she lowered her eyes. For a moment she looked as though she might say nothing more. Then, as if the warmth of the tea loosened her tongue, she spoke quietly.

"My family wouldn't see it that way."

Primrose tilted her head. "No?"

Maggie shook her head, curls bouncing. "I'm a Thistle. My father owned half the mills in Haworth before he died. Everyone expected me to be a lady of the house, not dusting shelves."

Primrose blinked, surprised. "Thistle?" She had not put it together before but now she remembered she had heard the name before, spoken in whispers of wealth and influence.

Maggie's voice grew smaller. "After Father's death, my mother shut herself away. She's not been seen in town for years. Folks say the grief hollowed her out." She stared into her tea, eyes distant. "So, I know what it is, miss. Losing a parent and being left with more questions than answers."

Primrose reached across the table, laying her hand lightly over Maggie's. "Then we do have something in common."

Maggie glanced up, eyes bright with the first flicker of trust.

For a moment, they sat together in silence, two women bound by loss and circumstance, sipping tea as the shop slowly came alive with morning light.

Primrose rose from her chair, smoothing the front of her apron as Maggie finished the last sip of her tea.

"Maggie," she said gently, "I'll be out for most of the day, running a few errands." She paused, as if weighing the words, then gave a small smile. "If it's agreeable to you, I'd like you to help me prepare for the reopening of the shop. Fresh flowers for the table, perhaps some fine tea and a few sweetmeats from the confectioner. Something to welcome our first guests properly."

Maggie's face lit up, her shyness momentarily forgotten. "Oh, I'd love to, miss. The shop will look fine, it will. I'll see to it."

Primrose reached into her pocket and drew out the shop key, pressing it into Maggie's palm with quiet solemnity. "Then it is yours to safeguard until I return. I'll be back before closing, and I trust you'll keep watch over the place."

Maggie's fingers curled protectively around the key, her chin lifting with a touch of pride. "You may count on me, Miss Eversley."

Primrose gave her hand a reassuring pat, then gathered her coat and stepped out into the morning mist.

The stone edifice of St. Michael's rose before her, its Gothic spire piercing the sky like a silent sentinel over Haworth. Time had weathered the sandstone into shades of honey and gray, and ivy crept in green veins across the lower walls. The great oak doors stood open, their iron hinges worn but sturdy.

Inside, candles flickered in wrought-iron sconces, their flames bending in the draft that seeped through narrow stained-glass windows. Hues of ruby, emerald, and sapphire spilled across the flagstones, fractured by the glass saints above.

A handful of parishioners knelt in scattered pews, murmuring prayers too soft to catch. Their whispers rose and fell with the sigh of the wind that seemed to seep even into this hallowed space. The hush was profound, broken only by the faint creak of wood and the distant toll of the clock tower outside.

Primrose tilted her head back, letting her eyes wander over the vaulted ceiling where ribs of stone crisscrossed like the frame of some divine tapestry. The craftsmanship, she thought, was as much a prayer as the words uttered below.

Her reverie was disturbed by the measured sound of footsteps echoing up the nave—slow, deliberate—drawing closer behind her.

The footsteps halted just behind her.

"Miss Eversley," came a voice—deep, warm, touched with the cadence of the pulpit.

She turned to find the parish priest regarding her with kind eyes; his face lined with the years of both care and consolation. He inclined his head, and when she extended her hand in greeting, he clasped it firmly in both of his, his palms warm despite the chill of the church.

"It has been far too long since the Eversley name graced these walls," he said softly. "Your father was once a familiar figure here."

Their hands lingered in the clasp a moment longer than formality required, something unspoken exchanged in the quiet glow of the candles.

She drew a breath, steadying herself. "Might I trouble you for a few moments in private, Father? There are matters on which I should value your counsel."

He studied her face—saw the strain behind her polite composure—and nodded gravely.

"Of course, my child. Come."

With a gentle gesture, he led her toward a side door beneath the choir loft, the hem of his cassock whispering against the stones as they moved out of the nave and into the cloistered hush of his study.

The study was small, paneled in dark oak, its single window cloaked by heavy drapery. The faint scent of beeswax and incense lingered in the air. A crucifix hung upon the wall above a clutter of parish ledgers.

The priest gestured for her to sit, and once they had both settled, he folded his hands upon the desk, his gaze steady and patient.

Primrose clasped her gloves in her lap, then spoke quietly, almost as if confessing.

"Father, I fear I must ask you of things I should have been present for but was not. My father's death—" She swallowed, steadying herself. "I was told only that it was sudden. I need to know what truly befell him. And... where he was laid to rest. It troubles me deeply that I was not here."

The priest's face softened. He leaned forward, his voice low.

"Your father's passing was indeed sudden." he said.

"Some whisper of mischance, others of darker deeds." He continued.

Primrose's chest tightened; she forced her breathing to remain even.

"As for his resting place," he continued gently, "your father lies in consecrated ground just beyond the east wall of the churchyard. A modest stone marks him, for there was no time to arrange more before winter came. I prayed the rites myself."

Her throat caught at the thought of her father buried in Haworth soil, alone.

The priest reached across the desk and laid a hand

briefly upon hers. "I feared you would carry a burden of absence, but know this—he was not alone in spirit. Many of the town came. He was respected, even by those who found his pursuits... unusual."

Primrose drew in a measured breath, her fingers tightening around the gloves in her lap.

"Father, forgive me if I trouble you further, but... may I ask who was present at his burial?" Her voice steadied as she went on. "I should like to thank them myself. It seems the least I can do, after my absence."

The priest regarded her thoughtfully, then gave a slow nod. "Of course. Your father had more friends than perhaps you knew. There was Isabel the baker, Ms. Crowley, the town historian, Mr. Fletcher from the butchery, Mr. Bramley the grocer, and several of the parish ladies who tend the flowers in the yard. Even a few men from the town council stood among us."

Primrose's breath caught in her throat as he went on.

The priest leaned back slightly, recalling. "Yes, and there were others you might wish to know. Dr. Thaddeus Bellamy, for one. He spoke kindly of your father, said his scholarship was not yet finished. He seemed... burdened, almost protective of your father's work."

Primrose's eyes flicked upward, sharp with interest. Bellamy—the name from Father's letters.

The priest went on, oblivious to her quickened breath. "And Rowan Ashcroft, of course. He was there with his ever-present notebook, standing at the edge as though both participant and observer. I confess I could not tell whether he came out of friendship or the promise of a story."

Primrose's lips curved in a polite smile, though tension coiled in her stomach. Ashcroft again. Always watching.

"And Harold Fenwick," the priest finished gently. "He lingered near the rear, said nothing, left before I could speak with him. A strange thing, though perhaps it was simply grief in his own way."

The name struck her like a blow, though her expression betrayed nothing.

Fenwick. She thought with contempt.

She inclined her head gracefully, though her thoughts roiled. "I see. Thank you, Father. It means much to know he was not unattended."

The priest smiled gently. "It was a small kindness, child. Your father was a man of mysteries, yes, but he was no outcast. You may be sure of that."

Primrose murmured her gratitude.

The churchyard was hushed, the morning mist clinging low to the grass. Primrose walked slowly, her boots sinking into the damp earth as she traced the neat rows of headstones until her eyes fell upon the name she dreaded and longed for in equal measure.

Alaric Eversley.

She knelt, her fingers brushing away dew and blades of grass from the carved letters. The cool stone steadied her trembling hand. Her heart ached in her chest, sharp and suffocating, yet she held her breath and let it crest like a wave.

As she leaned forward, something caught her eye— half-hidden beneath a scattering of twigs and wet leaves at the base of the headstone. She reached down and pulled it free.

An acorn.

She glanced about in confusion. No oak trees on the church grounds, not in the garden borders nor in the distant hedges. She turned the small thing in her palm, the cap still firm, the shell glossy black as though it had fallen only yesterday.

"Where did you come from?" she whispered, brows furrowed. The acorn felt warm against her skin— though perhaps that was only her imagination.

She slipped it carefully into her pocket, the weight strangely significant. Then, bowing her head, she breathed her words silently, lips barely moving.

Her chest rose and fell in a shudder as she pressed her hand flat to the stone, her eyes stinging with tears she would not let fall. A private reconciliation, carried only on the still air between them.

Primrose wandered through the crooked streets of Haworth, the folded map pressing against her side with every step. The town was stirring now, shopkeepers drawing up shutters, the scent of fresh bread carried from the baker's on the corner. Yet her thoughts remained on the acorn nestled in her pocket, heavy as a stone, insistent as a question she could not yet answer.

She scanned the lanes and yards, searching for the

unmistakable spread of oak branches. Hours might have passed—or only minutes—when she turned down a narrow road, one she did not remember walking before. The cottages leaned close, their windows shuttered, and just beyond them stood a single oak tree. But it was not any ordinary English oak tree.

Its broad trunk rose defiantly against the mottled sky, its branches spreading like arms across the cramped lane. She stopped short, heart jolting. This was no common planting. Its presence felt deliberate—guarded, almost—and it was the only oak she had yet seen within the town.

Her hand went instinctively to her pocket, brushing against the acorn she had taken from her father's grave.

Beneath its shade loomed a heavy wooden door set into the wall of an unmarked building. No sign hung above it, no merchant's mark painted on the lintel. The door was plain, save for the iron studs driven into its surface, and a small, square slide cut into its upper half. It looked less like a shop entrance and more like a threshold meant to keep the world at bay.

Primrose found herself drawn toward it, her curiosity tightening with each step. She wondered—
What sort of business needed no sign? What sort of people slipped in and out unseen?

She was only a few paces away when a voice called out behind her.

"Miss Eversley?"

She turned, and there stood Rowan Ashcroft.

His tone was smooth, even pleasant, but his sudden appearance in this quiet lane at this exact moment startled her. And his expression—an instant of surprise quickly shuttered behind his usual composure—told her she was not the only one caught somewhere she ought not be.

Primrose squared her shoulders, masking her startlement with poise. "Are you once again following a lead, Mr. Ashcroft? Or are you following me?"

His lips curved faintly, though his eyes flicked past her to the building at her back. "And you, Miss Eversley? Don't tell me you're lost. These alleys can be... unforgiving to the unacquainted."

Before she could reply, a faint rasp caught her ear.

Behind her, the small iron slide set into the heavy wooden door scraped open. A pair of bright gray eyes stared out—unblinking, assessing.

She turned instinctively, but just as quickly the slide snapped shut with a dull clang.

Her unease prickled the delicate hair on her arms. She lingered, staring at the door as though it might yield its secrets if she willed it hard enough.

Rowan stepped closer, his voice low and urgent. "Miss Eversley," he said, reaching gently for her arm. The warmth of his hand was at odds with the tension in his jaw. "There's something I want to show you. Not here."

Her hazel eyes searched his face, torn between suspicion and the sharp pull of curiosity. Finally, she gave the smallest nod.

Rowan released a measured breath, then inclined his head toward the end of the lane. "Come with me."

And, heart quickening, she did.

They walked in silence at first, the sound of their steps softened by the uneven cobbles. Primrose tried to steady her breath, though her mind was alive with questions about the door—and the eyes behind it.

Rowan guided her toward the edge of the square. At last, he stopped beneath the worn lintel of an apothecary, its painted sign faded to near illegibility.

He leaned one shoulder casually against the doorframe, but his voice carried a weight beneath its ease. "Your father wasn't only a shopkeeper of fine tomes. He kept... records. Journals, accounts, correspondences. Some say he was too curious for his own good."

Primrose crossed her arms, her chin lifting. "I've begun to suspect as much."

A ghost of a smile flickered at Rowan's lips. "Then perhaps you won't be surprised to learn he asked questions about certain gatherings in Haworth. Meetings held in places most never notice."

Her eyes lit up—she thought of the heavy wooden door and the eyes watching from within. "And you? Do you frequent such places?"

He held her gaze, unflinching but not answering. Instead, he reached into his coat pocket and drew out a folded scrap of paper, yellowed at the edges.

"A note," he said, offering it between two fingers.

"Written by your father's own hand. He mentioned a sigil—a flame within a pyramid, entwined with a dragon. He thought it tied to an order older than the town itself."

Primrose took the slip, her fingers brushing his. The words were written in her father's distinctive script. But there was something about the neatness, the convenient phrasing, that made her wonder if Rowan had given her everything—or only what he wished her to see.

She slipped it into her pocket, eyes narrowing. "You've given me another crumb, Mr. Ashcroft. But crumbs never tell the whole story."

His smile deepened, but his eyes flickered away as though shadows pressed close. "True. But sometimes crumbs keep you from stepping off a cliff."

He straightened, glancing at the square's clocktower. "I must leave you here. Deadlines don't wait, even in Haworth. Be careful, Miss Eversley."

And before she could press him further, he was gone—a man carrying more secrets than truths.

Primrose arrived back at the shop just as the last of the daylight bled into twilight, the streetlamps flaring to life one by one along the cobbles. She paused at the threshold, her gaze falling on the small but thoughtful touches Maggie had brought into the shop. A vase of fresh flowers stood proudly on the counter, their colors brightening the dark wood. A tin of fine tea and a box of sugared biscuits rested neatly beside them, wrapped in brown paper and tied with twine.

Primrose felt a swell of warmth—part pride, part relief. The shop, her father's shop, no longer looked shuttered or forgotten. It looked alive again.

Maggie appeared from between the shelves, a feather duster still in hand. "Do you approve?" she asked, her voice hopeful.

Primrose allowed herself a smile. "I do indeed. You've done splendidly, Maggie. Tomorrow the doors shall open properly again. I think Father would be pleased."

Maggie's face flushed. "I hoped to make it welcoming."

Together, they carried the tea and sweets to the pair of chairs by the window. They sat with steaming cups in hand, the scent of flowers mingling with the sharp bite of fresh brew. The town outside was quiet now, the last shoppers hurrying home, the square bathed in the mellow glow of lanterns

Their talk was easy—teasing comments about the dust that seemed to breed in corners, shared laughter over Maggie's harried attempts to barter with the baker for the last box of biscuits. The silliness softened them both, weaving a thread of companionship neither had realized they'd been missing.

For the first time since her arrival, Primrose felt something resembling readiness settle into her bones. Tomorrow, the bookshop would reopen. Tomorrow, she would welcome the world in.

But tonight, she allowed herself the comfort of tea, sweets, and the fragile but promising beginnings of friendship.

Later that evening, when Maggie had gone and the shop lay hushed beneath the settling dark, Primrose slipped upstairs to her father's study. The lamplight fell soft across the desk and shelves, the air tinged faintly with the scent of old paper and beeswax polish.

From her pocket she took the acorn, turning it once in her hand before setting it carefully upon the edge of a shelf—small, unassuming, yet impossibly out of place. She regarded it for a long moment, as though it might whisper its meaning if she stared hard enough.

Behind her, Athena shifted on her perch, feathers catching the glow like pale fire.

Primrose smiled gently and moved closer. *"Sweet dreams, darling,"* she murmured, as if the owl were both guardian and confidante.

Athena blinked once, slow and solemn, before tucking her head beneath a wing.

Satisfied, Primrose wandered down the hall to her own room. At last, it no longer felt borrowed. Her trunk had been unpacked, books stacked neatly on the small table, her dresses hanging in the wardrobe. A knitted shawl from her mother lay draped at the foot of the bed. The space was hers now—hers and no longer a shadow of his.

Yet as she sank onto the mattress, thoughts gathered like restless moths. Rowan Ashcroft— journalist, too curious by half. The door at the end of the lane with its strange silence, its oak tree standing sentinel. The uneasy feeling of being watched.

Primrose folded her hands in her lap, her mind slipping into its familiar order.

Gather information on Rowan Ashcroft. Inquire discreetly. Observe carefully.

Investigate the door at the end of the lane. Learn what lies beyond.

She exhaled slowly, committing the notes to memory. Tomorrow would bring its own revelations. Tonight, she would rest.

The morning dawned bright and clear, a fitting day for renewal. Primrose and Maggie carried the painted placard out to the cobbled street—Grand Reopening Today: Rare & Antiquarian Books, Curiosities, and More—its lettering careful, flourished, the handiwork of their shared effort the night before.

By midmorning, the bell above the door chimed steadily, ushering in a tide of visitors. The shop filled with the murmur of voices, the rustle of turning pages, and the faint scent of ink and leather mingling with Maggie's carefully arranged flowers.

A young curate in his black coat lingered reverently over a shelf of sermons and moral tracts, eyes bright with the earnest hunger of study.

A pair of schoolboys pressed together at the cabinet of travelogues, whispering in awe at the adventures of far-off lands—India, Africa, the New World.

A widow in bombazine silk asked softly after novels "to pass the long evenings," her voice carrying the edge of loneliness.

A gentleman farmer, boots still dusted with the fields, came in search of agricultural treatises—crop rotation, new tools from the continent, anything that might give him an edge. Beside him, his daughter craned toward the poetry shelf, cheeks flushed as she clutched a slim volume of Keats to her chest.

Even a seamstress, apron dusted with threads, stopped to finger the pages of a worn Shakespeare, whispering lines under her breath with quiet delight.

The air was alive with curiosity, with the joyful hum of learning and leisure mingling together. Coins clinked, books changed hands, and for the first time since her father's death, Primrose felt the shop alive again—her father's legacy pulsing in every corner.

Then the bell above the door rang once more, and the shift was immediate. The lively chatter dulled as though a cold draught had swept through.

A tall man stepped across the threshold. His coat was well-cut but severe, his boots polished to a sheen. He paused just inside, eyes sweeping the room with deliberate slowness, and though nothing in his manner was outwardly hostile, a knot formed low in Primrose's stomach.

She couldn't say why. Perhaps it was the stillness that clung to him, or the way the light from the doorway seemed reluctant to follow him in. Whatever it was, the pleasant hum of the morning dimmed to a strange hush.

Primrose forced her breath steady, smoothing her skirt as she crossed the room. She reminded herself she was the mistress of this place now, and it was her duty to greet every visitor with courtesy.

"Good day, sir," she said, voice calm but measured.

The man inclined his head slightly, his gaze resting on her with unnerving weight.

"Hello Primrose, I am Harold Fenwick.".

14 PRESSURES AND PROMISES

Harold Fenwick. She thought. The mysterious Mr. Fenwick. Why do you seem so familiar and yet so... dark.

She tried to remain calm and reserved. She smiled and said, "Pleasure to meet you."

"What a pleasure to see you settling in. Your father and I were... very close." She was sure he was lying but could not quite grasp why she felt it so.

Something in the way he lingered on the words made her uneasy.

Fenwick ambled closer, eyes skating over the shop as if he owned it. "I imagine you're eager to return to your post in New York, back to your modern comforts. Running a shop like this must feel rather provincial after the grand institutions you're accustomed to."

Her heart thudded. How does he know about that?

He leaned in slightly, lowering his tone. "I should like to help you, Miss Eversley. Spare you the burden of responsibility. Allow me to take this shop off your hands. A generous sum, of course, and all done quickly, discreetly."

Primrose's lips curved politely, though her chest grew cold. His words had the cadence of kindness, but each syllable pressed like a claw.

Before she could reply, the bell chimed again. Rowan Ashcroft stepped inside, coat collar turned up against the wind. The shift in Fenwick's expression was instant—a flicker of recognition, a curl of distaste.

"Well," Fenwick said briskly, already donning his hat again. "We shall discuss particulars another time. I'll have my assistant bring the necessary paperwork. But let us keep this matter... private. No need for all of

Haworth to chatter about it."

He tipped his hat with a false smile, then strode toward the door. As he passed Rowan, the two men's eyes locked. Rowan held his gaze evenly, not a word exchanged, but the tension between them was thick.

Primrose caught the moment, storing it carefully away. Fenwick vanished into the street.

Rowan turned his attention to her at last, his usual composure softened by curiosity. "Business negotiations, Miss Eversley?" he asked lightly, but his eyes searched hers with a keenness she did not miss.

She knew, now, where Fenwick got his information.

Primrose waited until the shop quieted again, then turned to Rowan with narrowed eyes. Without a word, she guided him past the front counter and into the shadowed alcove of the back shelves.

"How did you know," she asked in a low, precise voice, "that Fenwick was speaking to me about business?"

Rowan leaned lightly against the shelf, the picture of ease, though his eyes flickered. "A fair assumption, Miss Eversley. Fenwick owns half the enterprises in Haworth. Bought them up one by one. If he was here, it was bound to be for that reason."

She crossed her arms. "Convenient guesswork."

His brows rose, feigning offense. "You can check the library archives for records. It's all there black and white."

Then he scoffed and said, "Oh, wait... do you think I am spying on you?"

"I'm asking," she returned coolly.

He straightened, gaze steady. "No. Primrose." He gently took her hand and whispered, "I simply wanted to know you better. That's all."

Primrose's lips pressed thin. "Then why is it that wherever I turn—there you are? At the church. In the lanes. At my very door. You appear at every corner, Mr. Ashcroft. Surely even you see how it looks."

He allowed a soft laugh, though it rang a little too smooth. "Coincidence, nothing more. Haworth isn't so sprawling a place that our paths shouldn't cross. And, truth be told—" he lowered his voice, "I find your company rather compelling."

The words were meant to reassure, his tone warm, his expression sincere. And outwardly, she allowed her shoulders to ease.

But inside, suspicion coiled tight as wire. His timing, his answers, his practiced charm—he always had the right words. Too many of the right words.

Her expression softened, but behind her eyes a storm gathered. If Rowan Ashcroft thought he could charm her, he was mistaken. Whatever part he played in her father's death, she would uncover it—and him—piece by piece.

The next afternoon, she left the shop in the care of Maggie and went to the small library near the church. It had a slightly musty smell mixed with leather the kind of quiet sanctuary her father would have adored. Primrose slipped into the archives, a slim chamber at the back where the shelves bowed with bound volumes of the Haworth Gazette and assorted county ledgers.

She began with the name that had needled her most: Rowan Ashcroft.

Her fingers traced headlines, brittle newsprint crackling under her touch. At first glance, it only fueled her unease. "Secret Meetings in the Dales? By Rowan Ashcroft." "Unusual Shipments Vanish from Whitby Dockyards." His byline lurked beside every hint of conspiracy, as though he had been circling her father's world long before Alaric Eversley's death.

Her heart quickened. Was this his cover? Was he documenting the very deeds he was complicit in?

She leaned closer, lips pressed into a thin line, until a paragraph caught her eye.

When asked for comment, local antiquarian Alaric Eversley warned that "artifacts of great historical value have a way of slipping quietly into the wrong hands if men of conscience do not stand guard. The question, then, is whether Haworth has such men—or whether silence will prove its ruin."

Primrose froze. Her father's voice, recorded on the page—public, defiant, and paired with Rowan's pen.

Her suspicion began to crack. She turned page after page, chasing the threads. Rowan had not been shielding men like Fenwick. He had been exposing them—naming trades gone missing, hinting at secret societies cloaked in "charitable fraternities," pressing questions no one else dared voice.

Her pulse had been drumming with every line she read, expecting to find Rowan's fingerprints on her father's death. But instead, the truth unfurled like a knife pulled from shadow: Rowan had been circling the same darkness as her father, chasing it in print, daring to name what others only whispered.

The realization hit her hard, almost dizzying. He hadn't been her father's enemy—he had been his ally.

Primrose's hand hovered on the page, trembling slightly. If Rowan was digging this deep, then he wasn't just reporting. He was entangled. Perhaps willingly. Perhaps not. But a man who waded into such waters never came out clean.

She snapped the ledger shut, the sound sharp in the hushed room.

Next, she grabbed the town ledgers. It didn't take long. Harold Fenwick's name threaded through decades of records, never bold but always present. Quiet acquisitions of mills, textile shops, small holdings. Businesses that seemed to wither once his name was attached, their former owners vanished from the pages of Haworth life as though swallowed whole.

Primrose leaned closer, tracing dates with her fingertip. He hadn't just bought shops—he had absorbed them. And always, there were whispers—rumors of pressure, debts called in, signatures given under duress. No proof, never proof. Only patterns. As reported in the stories written by Rowan.

She turned a page, tracing her finger along a column of figures that grew bolder, riskier, in the years just before her father's death. Whatever business Fenwick ran, it was not the harmless trade of a gentleman collector.

Her hazel eyes narrowed. *If father had uncovered too much, it might explain why he was murdered. And if Fenwick wants to acquire yet another Haworth business, perhaps that is part of it.*

She sighed. *But why is he quietly acquiring all these businesses and then letting them dissolve? Why would any proper businessman do such a thing?*

Primrose closed the ledger carefully, a single curl slipping loose against her cheek. "Secrets and sums," she murmured. "All roads lead back to Fenwick."

She gathered her notes into her satchel, the worn leather creaking in protest. Tomorrow, she would follow the trail where numbers became names, and names became enemies.

For tonight, though, she wanted to check the shop's ledgers to find the connection with Fenwick and why he wants to take the shop off her hands so badly.

Somewhere in the distance, a clock tolled the hour.

Primrose rose from the table, with only one thought clear in her mind: *Harold Fenwick is no mere businessman.*

He was a man worth watching.

Primrose stepped out of the library into the deepening dusk. The cobbles of Main Street gleamed faintly in the mist, lanterns flickering to life one by one along the row of shops.

Her stomach growled in protest. She had eaten nothing since morning, too absorbed in ink-stained ledgers and fading headlines.

On impulse, she crossed to The Fox & Thistle, a modest inn where travelers and locals alike took their evening meals. The windows glowed amber, laughter spilling into the street. Inside, the air was warm with the aroma of roasted meats and herbs.

Clara Bellamy, the innkeeper, spotted her at once. "Miss Eversley! You've a look about you—like a woman who's stared too long at words today. Sit yourself down; I'll fetch you a plate."

Primrose smiled faintly, grateful for Clara's brisk kindness. She took a seat near the hearth, where a knot of townsfolk were trading gossip over their tankards.

It wasn't long before the name Fenwick drifted to her ears.

"Here you go love, I'm Clara Bellamy I run the inn, If you need anything else I will be right over by the fire."

Primrose smiled and thanked her.

"He's bought half the old mills, mark my words," muttered Horace Browning, the clockmaker. "And always through some shadow of a company—never his own hand."

Daisy Appleton, the florist, leaned in conspiratorially. "My cousin swears he saw crates delivered to Fenwick's house at midnight. Not cloth, not books—

something heavier."

The table erupted in speculation. Primrose kept her gaze fixed on the flames, her fork paused over her stew. Secrets followed Fenwick like a shadow, it seemed.

Primrose was nearing the end of her bowl and her stew was beginning to get cold but her mind was elsewhere, turning over what she had heard.

Numbers, shipments, whispers in taverns. The pattern was beginning to take shape.

The tavern door swung open with a gust of wind, and in stepped Rowan Ashcroft. He spotted her almost at once, his sharp gray eyes cutting through the dimness as though he had expected to find her here.

"Miss Eversley," he said smoothly, inclining his head before gesturing toward the empty chair at her table. "May I?"

Primrose hesitated only a moment before offering a polite smile. "Of course."

As he settled opposite her, the firelight catching in the handsome curves of his face, he added casually, "I saw you at the archives today."

Her brows lifted. "Did you?" She had seen no one.

"I was working in the back rooms. A different collection." He stirred the steam from his teacup, almost too casually. "Research of my own."

She tilted her head, studying him. "Tell me, Mr. Ashcroft—are you a member of some secret society bent on taking over the town?"

He let out a short, nervous laugh, then leaned in, dropping his voice to a conspiratorial whisper. "Shhh. Don't tell anyone."

His gray eyes flicked up to hers, searching, as though measuring how serious she truly was.

Primrose gave a nervous laugh of her own, though her words came plain and sharp. "I am searching for my father's killer." She set down her fork, meeting his gaze squarely. "What do you know about Harold Fenwick?"

The merriment of the room seemed to dim around them. Rowan's expression sobered, the easy charm fading like smoke.

"Enough," he said at last, his voice low. "Too much, perhaps. But not here." His glance shifted toward the nearby tables, where townsfolk still murmured and laughed. "Fenwick has ears everywhere."

Primrose lowered her gaze to her bowl and forced herself to take a few more bites, though her appetite had fled. The stew was rich with rosemary and barley, but each mouthful tasted faintly of ash beneath the weight of Rowan's words.

He waited, patient, sipping his tea as though the air between them were not tightening like a drawn bowstring.

At last, she set down her fork. "Very well," she said quietly. "This isn't the place."

Rowan arched a brow, the faintest smile tugging at his lips. "No?"

She glanced toward the laughing townsfolk, then back at him. "No. If you truly know something about Fenwick—if you truly wish to speak of my father—then you'll come with me. To the shop."

For a moment he searched her face again, as though weighing the sincerity in her hazel eyes. Then he rose smoothly, offering his arm in that practiced Edwardian fashion, though his voice carried a touch of irony. "Lead on, Miss Eversley. Your father's shadow seems to linger in every corner of this town. Perhaps tonight we chase it together."

Primrose slipped her satchel over her shoulder, the folded notes from the archives pressing against her side. She cast one last glance at the inn's warm hearth before stepping out into the mist. The night air was cool, heavy with the scent of coal smoke and damp earth.

At her side, Rowan kept pace, silent but watchful.

Toward the waiting shop they walked—toward dust, locked doors, and the secrets her father had left behind.

The lamps in the shop cast a soft amber glow, flickering against the spines of books that lined the shelves like silent witnesses. Primrose poured the tea, the china rattling faintly as she set the cups on the small table by the front window.

It was their usual spot, though the curtains now hung drawn against the night. The world outside was shut away; only shadows remained within.

Rowan sat back in the worn chair opposite her, his profile etched in lamplight. For a moment he simply stirred his tea, the silver spoon clinking in steady rhythm. Then he set it aside and lifted his gaze.

"There is something you should know," he said at last. His voice, low and deliberate, carried a weight that gave the very air a heaviness. "Something of Fenwick. And of your father."

Primrose held her breath, her fingers tightening on the porcelain handle.

Rowan leaned forward, elbows resting on his knees. "Fenwick was no mere trader. There are shipments—crates that slip into Haworth by night—they carry more than books and textiles. They carry things men were never meant to own." He paused, as if the words themselves strained against his tongue. "Artifacts. Objects with... properties. Your father sought to keep them safe. Fenwick sought to use them. He has a distorted vision of how they should be used."

"Used? Used for what?" she asked.

Rowan pressed his lips firmly together before he spoke his next words. "To save the world."

"What? What do you mean? Why tell me this now?" she whispered.

Rowan's mouth curved in something like a bitter smile. "Because loyalty is a brittle thing when one begins to doubt the cause. And I..." He stopped, shaking his head, as though brushing aside thoughts better left unsaid. "You deserve at least this truth."

He rose abruptly.

She stood and said, "Rowan—wait—", following him, confused.

But he was already at the door, his coat drawn tight.

She grabbed his hand and held it. He refused to look in her eyes.

"Loyalty is extremely brittle," she said, "and if you want me to trust you then tell me what it is—what are you afraid to tell me?"

His face was stern as he turned, looked her in the eyes and said, "If you're looking for trouble, Primrose, look closer to home."

Without another word, he slipped into the foggy street. Through the glass she glimpsed his figure melt into the shadows, hugging walls and alleys as though hunted—or hunting still.

Primrose remained frozen in her chair, the cooling tea untouched before her. The silence of the shop pressed in, her father's secrets stirring restlessly around her.

Whatever Rowan Ashcroft was, he was no simple ally. And now, more than ever, Fenwick's name burned in her mind like a brand.

Save the world from what? Or whom?

15 TRUTH HIDES IN PLAIN SIGHT

Her father's study smelled of old paper and pipe smoke, though the man himself had been gone these many months. Primrose closed the door behind her, shutting out the creaks and whispers of the shop, and crossed to the heavy desk. The lamplight spilled across its scarred surface, a familiar battlefield where her father had once fought with ink, maps, and mysteries.

She placed the scrap of paper Rowan had given her at the center. Its creased edges and faded scrawl seemed suddenly weightier in the hush of the room.

One by one, she laid out the rest of her clues like evidence in a trial:

the map, its corners curling from age
the jeweled compass, gleaming and restless
the black acorn
the mysterious book, its spine cracked, pages bristling with cryptic annotations

She added her own notes, pages filled with hurried script, observations from the archives, and lists of Fenwick's transactions. The iron keys clinked softly as she set them beside the box, its lid closed but humming with unspoken promise.

From her perch upon a stack of books, Athena blinked her amber eyes and gave a low, solemn hoot, as if blessing the work.

Primrose drew a breath and leaned over the desk, hands splayed on either side of the assembled relics.

"Let us see," she murmured, her voice barely louder than the ticking of the clock on the mantel.

Her gaze traveled from the compass to the map, from the acorn to Rowan's scrap of paper. Each piece seemed a thread, and somewhere in the tangle was a pattern her father had once seen—had died for, perhaps.

She spoke the thoughts as they came, as if saying them aloud might coax them into shape:

"The compass points not north, but to what is needed. The acorn... a seed, a beginning. The map—routes to what? A spiral deep in the moors, a spiral staircase, a spiral key and secrets buried beneath them. Rowan's note—cryptic, withheld. The missing book—why hide it unless it contains what others seek? And you, my darling Athena—hiding in a chamber with only a small window to come and go unnoticed."

She sat back, brow furrowed. Athena shifted to her perch, feathers ruffling as if impatient.

Primrose pressed her fingers to the keys, cold iron biting into her skin. "Doors within doors. My father left more locked away than I have yet dared to open."

The lamp flickered, shadows bending across the desk. And for a moment, she thought she almost saw it—the faint outline of a path linking object to object, as though the pieces themselves longed to be assembled into a truth.

Primrose's hand stilled over her notes.

The jeweled compass, quiet until now, gave a sudden tremor. Its needle quivered, then began to whirl in frantic circles, the tip flashing in the lamplight.

Primrose reached out, her pulse quickening, and lifted the compass in her hand. The metal was cool, almost cold, trembling faintly against her palm. Slowly—deliberately—the spinning slowed, the needle jerking as though resisting some unseen current. Then, with sudden certainty, it swung and locked into place.

It pointed—not to north, not to the scattered papers or the keys—but outward. Toward the shop itself.

Primrose followed its line, her eyes narrowing on the door that led back into the darkened bookstore.

Athena gave another soft call, feathers shivering as though in agreement.

Primrose tightened her grip on the compass. "So it's here," she whispered. "The answer isn't in my notes, nor the archives. It's in this shop."

The owl blinked solemnly, as if to say she had only just begun to scratch at the truth her father had buried.

The compass quivered in her hand as Primrose rose from the desk. Her eyes flicked to the door leading back to the shop, the needle fixed unwaveringly upon it. She grabbed the spiral key and put it in her pocket. Then she looked at Athena and asked, "Shall we?"

She crossed the study in two strides and turned the glass doorknob. The mechanism gave a reluctant click, and as the door swung open, Athena spread her wings in a sudden rush of air.

With a sharp cry, the owl was desperate to get out of the living quarters, her tawny-and-white feathers brushing Primrose's cheek as she opened the door and Athena swept into the darkened shop.

Primrose clutched the compass tight and hurried after her.

The shop was hushed, the only sound the faint rustle of wings above. Athena circled once, then dipped low, gliding through the shadows with purpose, as though she had flown this path a hundred times before.

The compass vibrated in Primrose's palm, its jeweled needle aligned with the owl's flight.

"Athena..." she called.

She found the bird, at last, at the top of a tall bookcase near the far wall, her talons curling around the carved wood. She bobbed her head once, sharp and deliberate, her gaze fixed downward.

Primrose slowed, the hair at the nape of her neck prickling. The compass's needle quivered, then stilled—pointing directly at the shelf beneath Athena's watch.

With reluctant hands she began pulling volumes down one by one, running her fingers along their spines, their brittle pages whispering as she checked for hidden slips. Maggie had spent countless hours restoring and ordering these shelves, and her guilt was heavy but Primrose spoke aloud as she shifted careful stacks aside.

"I'll put everything back," she promised softly to the empty shop.

Book after book yielded nothing but dust and disappointment. Her heart sank with each fruitless attempt.

Until at last her hands fell upon a heavy tome: A Rare Encyclopedia of Garden Flowers. The leather was worn, the gilt title nearly faded. She opened it with weary resignation, flipping through stiff pages filled with delicate illustrations—roses, foxgloves, violets.

Then she froze.

Her own name stared back at her in ink darker than the printed type. Primrose.

Her fingers trembled as she turned the page. Folded papers were pressed neatly between images of primrose blossoms, the paper yellowed but intact.

She unfolded it, breath shallow.

Hand drawn. What is this? Some kind of detailed sketches. But of what? She thought as she studied the drawings. Then, something in particular caught her eye. *What's this?*

Athena hooted once, low and steady.

"Yes! I see it now." She said aloud. The window Athen a used to access the hidden chambers below the shop. She began to recognize the shapes of the arches, the beams of the ceilings in the drawings before her.

Primrose pressed the paper to her chest. Her father's secrets were no longer whispers or shadows.

"These drawings are old. And they're not in father's handwriting." she said to Athena.

"If father didn't build them, then they were here when he acquired this shop. But who built them and why?" She looked at Athena and then whispered.

"Harold Fenwick has been acquiring businesses, then letting them fall to waste." A look of curiosity came over her and her expression showed she was deep in thought.

"Why would a businessman buy a building and then abandon it?" She looked back at Athena who bobbed her head as if Primrose were onto something.

Primrose suddenly got it. She took a deep excited breath and blurted out, "Because he's looking for something!"

Primrose stood up from the floor where she had been sitting and paced. "He's been buying the buildings because he's looking for the chambers. But how does he know they even exist?"

She let out a sigh and paced some more...until the sound of a loose floorboard grabbed her attention. She stopped at once and pushed on It with her foot. *Are you innocently or deliberately loose?*

She decided to see if there was a tool behind the shop's counter that she could pry it up with.

Frustrated, she ran upstairs and grabbed a butter knife. Upon her return she found the compass pointing directly at the floorboard and Athena waiting patiently on the books she had stacked on the floor.

She used the knife to pry the board loose bending the butter knife into a mangled mess in the process. What she found only deepened the mystery.

Chain of Title She read the words on the first document. *These look like conveyance documents.*

"1500s, it's in Latin. Peder Andresen. Given the 10th day of May, in the 15th year of the reign of King Henry VII." She looked at the other documents each in turn as she pulled them from the floor.

Then she came to one that was dated 1857. "Alaric Eversley and...my grandfather, Jerome Eversley."

A family heirloom of sorts. she thought to herself. *Are these men all relatives? If so, why have I never heard these names?*

She replaced the floorboard and put all the books back the way she found them. Then she gathered her new clues and headed back upstairs.

As Athena settled on her perch, Primrose hid the compass once again then went straight to the bedroom with the deeds. She placed them on the bedside table and slid herself into bed, under warm covers.

She thought back to her meal at the inn and how Rowan suddenly appeared. *How is it that man always finds me?* Then another memory tugged at her thoughts—the innkeeper Clara Bellamy—*Bellamy...the man father said he trusted near...where was it? Dr. Thaddeus Bellamy.* She pushed herself out of the bed, heart pounding. "I need to find him." she said to herself as she went to her father's office in search of her father's letter.

She scanned the letter for the town he mentioned. "Settle". She smiled as if relieved. "Well, that settles it."

The thought became a decision almost at once. Settle was a half day's travel by train. If she left in the morning, she could reach Settle before dusk, spend the night, and return the following day with answers— or at least with direction.

"How do I find a man I've never met? I don't know what he looks like and I can't inquire openly about him." She muttered to herself. "I wonder if Clara is trustworthy."

She looked at Athena and said, "It's a dilemma. I'll need to take a chance I think and hope for the best."

Athena fluttered down from the perch. Primrose bent, smoothing the owl's feathers gently. "Watch over the shop while I'm gone. Keep it safe for me."

She packed a small bag then readied herself for bed. She fell asleep quickly. Athena kept watch over her all night.

The night fog clung to the cobbles like damp wool, muffling the sound of boots and wheels. Rowan Ashcroft lingered in the shadows of a narrow alley, his coat drawn close, his breath pale in the cold air.

Before him, men moved like silhouettes across the lamplit yard, heaving crates from the back of a wagon. They worked quickly, silently—goods unloaded at an hour when no respectable trade should be done. The crates bore no markings, save for strange symbols burned faintly into the wood.

Rowan's eyes narrowed. He had seen these symbols before, though he had never spoken of them aloud.

The wagon creaked as another heavy box was set upon the ground. From the corner of the yard rose the dark bulk of a building he knew too well: a low structure with a heavy wooden door, tucked beneath the spreading arms of the old oak tree.

The door creaked open. A figure stepped out, broad-shouldered and unmistakable even in the gloom.

"Mr. Ashcroft."

Harold Fenwick's voice carried low but clear across the yard. His tone was not a request but an order. He gestured with a gloved hand toward the open door. "Inside."

Rowan hesitated, his face shadowed, unreadable. Then, with the ease of a man accustomed to playing two parts at once, he stepped from the alley and crossed the yard, his boots whispering against the stones.

The wooden door yawned open wider, swallowing him into the darkness beneath the oak.

And then it shut, sealing whatever business lay

within away from prying eyes.

As the wooden door groaned shut behind Rowan, sealing out the fog and lantern light, he air inside was thick with dust and something sharper—oil, perhaps, or smoke.

A single lamp hung from a beam overhead, its glow falling across stacks of crates, each branded with the same faint symbols he had glimpsed outside. The room smelled of earth and age, as though what lay inside those boxes had been buried long before finding its way here.

Fenwick stood near the center, gloved hands clasped behind his back. His eyes glittered with satisfaction.

"You're late," he said.

"I prefer to observe before I commit," Rowan replied evenly.

Fenwick's mouth curved, though it was not a smile. "Ever the cautious one. No matter. You'll see soon enough."

He gestured, and two men pried open the lid of a nearby crate. Rowan leaned closer despite himself. Inside lay not books, not textiles, but something far stranger: fragments of carved stone wrapped in burlap, their edges etched with symbols older than any scripture he knew.

"Artifacts," Fenwick said softly, almost reverently. "Pieces of the old world. Power buried, now brought to light." His eyes flicked to Rowan. "Power your friend Eversley sought to deny us. Power his daughter will never keep from me."

Rowan's jaw tightened, though he forced his expression to remain impassive.

Fenwick stepped closer, lowering his voice. "I know you've seen her. Spoke to her, even. Be careful, Ashcroft. Curiosity is a fine trait for a journalist. It is fatal in our work."

Rowan inclined his head, though his stomach churned. "Understood."

Fenwick turned away, signaling for the men to reseal the crate. "Good. Then we will speak further when the shipment is complete. For now—watch, and learn."

Rowan stood rigid in the lamplight, his thoughts a storm. He had come too far to turn back—but with every word Fenwick spoke, he felt the brittle weight of his allegiance begin to crack.

Rowan stood motionless as the lid thudded back into place, the sound echoing like a coffin nailed shut.

Fenwick moved among the crates with quiet command, his men obeying without question. Shadows stretched long across the walls, swallowing faces, swallowing truth.

Fenwick removed an object from a crate, opened the burlap It was wrapped In and smiled. Rowan could not see what it was but Fenwick wrapped it carefully and placed it in his pocket and left the room.

Rowan kept his expression steady, the careful mask of a man who belonged. Inside, his thoughts raced— each word, each symbol, each fragment of stone etching itself into memory.

But he did not move. Not yet.

He only watched. And listened.

And waited.

The next morning the train lurched forward with a hiss of steam, the countryside sliding past in blurred patches of green and gray. Primrose sat by the window, gloved hands folded over her satchel, the steady clatter of wheels beneath her matching the rhythm of her thoughts.

She briefly recalled her early morning conversation with Clara Bellamy. She'd stopped by the inn at dawn in the hopes of catching Clara alone. "Oh, yes love." she said, "He's my brotha. Why you lookin' for 'im?" Primrose hoped she was believable when she said she was looking for new curiosities for the shop. If not, she might need to be careful on the two-mile walk from the town to Victoria Cave where Clara said she'd find him. She even gave her a pair of knickerbockers and some boots for the hike. "You'll be needing these." Clara mused.

The train's whistle startled Primrose from her thoughts. As her focus resumed on the landscape she saw a lovely river. She watched as it snaked its way through the countryside.

"The compass points to the shop," she murmured under her breath.

The acorn, small and unassuming, yet now heavy with implication.

She thought of Rowan's words, of his hesitance in the shop.

"What am I missing?" she whispered.

The train whistled, plunging into a curve. Primrose pressed her forehead lightly against the cool glass, watching the Yorkshire countryside unfurl toward Settle. Yet nothing felt settled in her heart, in her mind. Somewhere ahead, Dr. Thaddeus Bellamy waited—her father's trusted confidant, a man who might finally stitch these loose threads into a tapestry she could understand.

Until then, all she could do was sift through clues in her head, again and again, as the train carried her deeper into the mystery her father had left behind.

The train rocked gently, the countryside blurring past, when a shadow fell across her table.

She glanced up. A tall stranger stood in the aisle, his hat brim pulled low, his coat collar turned against the chill. In his hand he held a slim book, its cover worn smooth from years of use.

Without preamble, he set it upon her table.

"You look like your mum," he said softly.

Primrose, startled, gasped for a moment then said "I beg your pardon—?"

But the man tipped his hat and stepped back, his face already lost in the swirl of passengers shifting for the platform. Within moments, the train shuddered to a halt at the Gargrave station, and he was gone— vanished into the throng on the platform without another glance.

Heart racing, Primrose pulled the book toward her. It was a faded volume of poetry, the spine cracked, the gilt nearly worn away. She opened the cover.

There, in her father's hand, was a line of script she had never seen before.

She quietly read It to herself. "Truth hides in plain sight, for those who remember where to look."

Primrose pressed the book to her chest, her eyes stinging. *Who was this stranger? How did he known my mother? And how has this book—my father's book— found its way to me?*

The train lurched forward again, carrying her onward. But the mystery now sat heavier in her heart.

Her father's secrets were no longer hers alone to chase. Others were watching. Others remembered.

Primrose's fingers trembled as she opened the book wider, thumbing through brittle pages. The poems were familiar—lines she had once overheard her father recite in the quiet of the shop. Robert Browning, his dramatic monologues full of hidden meanings.

But near the center, she paused.

There, scrawled faintly in the margin, was a symbol she knew.

She closed the book slowly, the image seared into her thoughts. The society was everywhere—in trade, in whispers, even hidden in books of verse.

She tightened her grip on the worn cover, her mind circling her father's warning. Truth hides in plain sight.

The train screeched to a halt, steam curling into the chill Yorkshire air. Primrose stepped down onto the platform, adjusting her satchel and drawing her cloak tighter. The town bustled with carts, horses, and the chatter of the townsfolk.

She paused, uncertain which road to take.

She turned to see a man atop a small carriage, reins in hand. His cheeks were ruddy from the cold, his smile broad. "Can I take you to the inn love?"

Primrose hesitated, then nodded. "Yes, Thank you."

The carriage jolted forward, the horse trotting briskly. The driver was talkative, filling the silence with rambling anecdotes about the weather, the crowds, and his neighbors back in Haworth.

"You're from Haworth?" Primrose asked, feigning polite curiosity.

"Aye, born and bred. My father had a shop there, years ago. Hard worker, he was. But the place—gone now." He shook his head, clucking his tongue. "Burned to the ground. Terrible shame. And all after some rich fellow bought him out. Can't recall the name, but I heard they tore up the floors before it went up in smoke—like they were searching for something."

Suddenly, he had Primrose's attention, but she kept her expression carefully neutral. "How dreadful," she murmured.

He nodded solemnly. "Aye. Shame for my father's work, all lost. Shops don't grow overnight, you know—they're planted, tended. Years to build." He sighed, then brightened, launching into another story about his wife's apple preserves and the lads who found massive bones in the cave in the hills out of town. "You believe they found a hippopotamus here, in England?"

Primrose only half-listened, her fingers tightening around her satchel that now contained the volume of poetry. If the man was right, the society had not only infiltrated Haworth—they had destroyed part of it in their search for the chambers.

Before she could press him for more, the carriage turned a final corner and drew up before the inn. Townsfolk streamed in and out, their chatter lively and unconcerned.

"There you are, miss," the driver said cheerfully.

She handed him the fare with a polite thank-you, though her mind was already racing ahead.

Primrose squared her shoulders and stepped through the door of the inn.

After securing a room for the night, she wandered about the town, getting her bearings and inquiring about the cave.

The next morning, she went downstairs and ate breakfast. Black pudding, bacon, eggs, and fried bread, hearty enough to sustain her for the day's journey.

Back In her room, she changed Into the borrowed knickerbockers and boots and headed out a side path near the river.

Somewhere out there was a cave and Dr. Thaddeus Bellamy—and, perhaps, the answers her father had meant her to find.

16 CAVE OF CURIOSITIES

As she meandered along with the river, she delighted in the flora and fauna of the area. Heather and magpies, and to her surprise a small tortoiseshell butterfly was flitting about. As she made her way up to the limestone crags, she could see purple saxifrage and just before she reached the caves--a red fox. She was so delighted she sat for a moment and just watched him.

A voice from behind her said, "Are you looking for me?" Startled, she turned around and said, "Oh dear you've given me a fright. I thought I was alone."

She asked if he was Dr. Bellamy. To that he answered, "Yes. and you must be looking for me because I'm the only one here."

"Well, aren't we all just fragments waiting to be unearthed?" She smiled as stood to shake his hand.

He was caught off guard for a moment but then he said, "I don't believe it. Primrose?"

"You know me?" She said hopeful.

"You are the spitting image of yer mum." He replied. To that she smiled with relief.

"Come, we'll go to my camp." and with that he motioned her to follow him.

When they reached the camp, she took it all in. Tents for sleeping and cooking, a wagon and a few horses. Pickaxes, shovels, hand trowels and brushes lay in orderly fashion with tables of sketch books and artifacts: ceramic shards, roman coins, and bones.

And in a larger tent were Bellamy's private quarters, presumably where he did his best thinking because there was a makeshift desk, a couple of simple chairs, candles, books, and a photograph. It was Dr. Bellamy, younger but unmistakable, standing beside crumbling temples in Egypt.

Primrose's breath caught in her throat There—standing at Bellamy's side—was her father. Alaric Eversley, his expression serious, his hands gripping scrolls or maps, as though caught mid-discovery.

Her father stood shoulder to shoulder with a cluster of men she did not recognize, their eyes sharp and knowing, their postures too formal for mere colleagues.

And then she saw it. Her hand rose instinctively to her mouth.

Harold Fenwick. He was younger but his features were unmistakable.

Primrose's knees weakened, and she gripped the edge of a table for balance.

The photograph whispered of a life her father had lived beyond the bookshop, beyond her childhood. And of a bond between him and Dr. Bellamy that ran far deeper than she had realized.

Dr. Bellamy regarded her closely. "I know why you're here."

Primrose swallowed hard, her heart thudding.

"Before we begin," Bellamy continued, his tone grave, "there's something you should know. Your mother taking you to America—it wasn't by chance. Your father insisted. He believed you'd both be safer across the ocean, far from Haworth."

Primrose felt the tears prick at the corners of her eyes, and fear rising with them, but she forced both back, steadying her breath. "I understand," she said quietly. "Thank you for telling me."

Her voice sharpened with determination. "Do you know what happened to him?"

Bellamy's face clouded with sadness. He hesitated, then said, "Have you heard of the Brotherhood of the Flame?"

Dr. Bellamy leaned back in his chair. Light streaming on his face from the sun drifting in through canvas flaps tied neatly on the tent.

"The Brotherhood of the Flame," he said at last, "is older than you might imagine. They cloak themselves in respectability—merchants, scholars, men of influence. But beneath the surface, they are united by one purpose: the pursuit of objects of power. Relics scattered through history. Your father and I... we spent years trying to keep such things out of their hands."

He gestured toward the photograph. "We traveled the world—your father, myself, and others—hunting down artifacts through lore and legend until we found the majority of them. Some we locked away. Others we returned to the earth. But the Brotherhood was always close behind. They believe these objects are keys to dominion—over knowledge, over wealth, over men's very spirits."

Primrose clutched her satchel tighter, the compass within seeming suddenly heavier.

Bellamy's eyes darkened. "Your father was one of the best among us. He had a gift for seeing patterns where others saw chaos. He uncovered that the Brotherhood had planted men in Haworth—quietly, patiently, weaving themselves into the fabric of the town. When he refused to bend to them, he became their enemy. He knew the danger, but he could not turn aside."

Primrose's throat ached, but she managed, "So... he was killed for what he knew?"

Bellamy nodded slowly. "It is the only conclusion I can reach. His death bore the marks of Brotherhood justice—silent, swift, and merciless."

Silence pressed between them.

"I keep that picture with me to remind me what we've been fighting for." He said at last.

He leaned forward, his voice gentler now. "Primrose, I must tell you plainly: the objects your father hid are not trinkets. The Brotherhood will stop at nothing to claim the rest. And if they discover that you have inherited his work, you will be in as grave a danger as he was."

Primrose met his gaze, her eyes burning. Fear trembled in her chest, but beneath it flickered something else—resolve.

"My father left me his clues," she said softly. "And I will follow them. The Brotherhood will not have what he died to protect."

Bellamy's expression softened with something like pride, though sorrow lingered there too. "Then you are your father's daughter, indeed."

Primrose set her satchel on the edge of Bellamy's desk with a soft thump. Her hands trembled as she loosened the clasp and pulled free—the jeweled compass.

He let out an excited gasp and reached for it, pausing briefly to ask permission.

"May I?" he asked.

She placed it in his hands. He examined it gently admiring every inch of it.

Bellamy drew the compass closer, the jewel at its center catching the sunlight. He turned it slowly in his hand, as though reacquainting himself with an old adversary.

"You must have questions," he said at last. "I will tell you what I can. Your father and I retrieved it together, more than thirty years ago, in Persia."

Primrose leaned forward, as if she was ready to hear a tale of adventures.

"It was said to belong to an ancient order of navigators—men who charted not just seas and deserts, but destinies. The compass does not point north. It points to what is sought—sometimes a person, sometimes a truth, sometimes a place. Dangerous in the wrong hands, invaluable in the right."

He set it gently on the desk, the needle quivering faintly. "We went there to see the Behistun Inscription—a carving in cliff commissioned by King Darius around 520 BC. What we found was much more. It's really where our journey and our quarrel with the Brotherhood began."

"We learned of location of the compass through a fragment of a manuscript, half-rotted and half-mad with superstition. But your father believed it. We journeyed deep into the desert, to ruins swallowed by sandstorms. It was there, hidden in a collapsed chamber, guarded by inscriptions warning of fire and betrayal."

Bellamy's gaze drifted, as if the memories flickered just beyond the limestone cliffs. "The Brotherhood sent men to follow us. These three, here, in this photo. We clashed with them beneath those ruins, among fallen stones and dust. Only one walked away." His jaw tightened. "And he carried scars enough to remember us by."

Primrose's pulse quickened, a chill running through her veins.

"Your father," Bellamy continued, his voice softer now, "was the one who claimed it. Harold Fenwick is the one who lived. He walks with a cane now thanks to your father."

He looked at her directly. "Alaric grew worried in his last years. He feared the Brotherhood's reach had spread farther than we imagined—that even in Haworth, their shadow lingered."

He sighed, "When he told me he saw Fenwick in town, he knew it was only a matter of time. He must have left it with you, Primrose, because he believed you were strong enough to carry what he no longer could."

Primrose lowered her gaze to the compass. It no longer seemed a curiosity from her father's shop. It seemed alive, pulsing faintly with purpose, the echo of her father's choices and sacrifices embedded within it.

Primrose hesitated only a moment before unfastening her satchel. "There's something else." she said.

Thaddeus looked at her curiously.

"On the train at the stop in Gargrave, a man passed me this and said I look like my mother." She continued, "I didn't get a good look at him and he was gone as quickly as he came."

Bellamy stood to receive the book and studied it with grave interest. He paced, lost in thought, his hands sifting through the pages as if he might find fragments of Alaric's life.

And then it happened.

The compass gave a sudden, violent shudder, its needle spinning wildly as though caught in a storm. Both of them froze.

Primrose's heart beat faster as the needle stilled— not toward north, nor toward the map, but toward Bellamy himself.

More precisely, to his hand. She had not noticed it before.

Primrose's eyes widened. Etched into his skin, was a faded tattoo: the spiral leading into flame.

The very sigil she had seen at the church, in her fathers sketches, in the hidden recesses of the staircase. The very mark of the Brotherhood.

"Dr. Bellamy..." she whispered, her voice trembling. "What is that?"

Bellamy drew his hand back slowly, curling it into a fist. His expression was unreadable, caught between shame and sorrow.

"It is a mistake," he said at last, voice low and unsteady. "A choice I made long ago, when I thought the Brotherhood could be... guided. Controlled." He looked up at her, his eyes stark with honesty. "Your father knew. He forgave me, though I've never forgiven myself. But Primrose—make no mistake—the compass does not lie. It sees what we try to bury. And it will always point to the truth."

Primrose's heart hammered, but she kept her hands still in her lap, her expression carefully composed. Inside, fear coiled like a snake—but she would not let him see it strike.

Bellamy drew a long breath, lowering himself slowly into his chair.

"I was a younger man when they found me," he began, his voice low. "The Brotherhood of the Flame promised knowledge—lost histories, forgotten truths, treasures hidden beneath the earth. For an archaeologist, such promises are intoxicating." His lips thinned. "I believed I could walk among them, take what I needed, and turn it toward good. But the Flame does not share its fire without burning what it touches."

He glanced down at the tattoo, flexing his hand as though the mark itself still burned him. "Your father was the one who pulled me back. He saw the Brotherhood for what it truly was—greed clothed in ritual, destruction masked as revelation. He gave me a choice: continue down their path, or stand with him against it. I chose to stand with your father."

Primrose pressed her palms against her skirt, fighting to steady her breath. "And they let you go?"

"No," Bellamy said flatly. "Men do not leave the Brotherhood. They watch me still, though I keep to shadows, moving carefully. Your father vouched for me. Without him, I suspect I would have been silenced long ago."

His eyes met hers then, sharp and pleading. "That is why I must warn you, Primrose. You carry not only his legacy but his enemies. The Brotherhood does not forget. And if they know you hold the compass..." He shook his head grimly. "They will not stop until it is theirs."

Primrose swallowed hard. She had feared betrayal, feared secrets—but not this: her father's closest friend marked by the very order that had likely killed him.

And yet, instead of recoiling, she leaned forward slightly, her voice steady despite the tremor in her chest. "Then tell me everything you know about them. Every weakness, every name, every place. If I am to finish what my father began, I cannot afford shadows any longer."

Bellamy's gaze softened, pride glinting faintly behind the sorrow. "You are his daughter, through and through."

Thaddeus leaned back in his chair, his eyes fixed on the compass still pointing toward his scarred forearm. He let the silence stretch before speaking, as if weighing whether this was the moment to unburden himself fully.

"You asked me to tell you everything," he said at last. "Then I will. But know this, Primrose: once spoken, these names will not leave your thoughts. You will see them in every shadow, in every whisper on the street. That is the Brotherhood's way."

Primrose nodded, her hands tightening in her lap. "Tell me anyway."

He drew a breath, his voice sinking lower.

"The Brotherhood of the Flame is not a single circle but many—threads woven across trade, scholarship, and faith. Their leaders call themselves the Keepers of the Flame. Each guards a secret, each pursues power in his own way. They believe the objects we sought—your compass among them—are keys to dominion over both the seen and unseen."

His eyes grew distant, haunted. "I stood among them once. I only knew one man. That is, until the men in Persia."

He raised a finger, counting them off.

"Harold Fenwick. A merchant with hands in every dishonest trade. Ruthless, clever, a man who cloaks greed in respectability. He will stop at nothing."

Primrose swallowed hard. She had suspected as much, but to hear it confirmed made her skin prickle.

"We did some digging to learn who the others were. Mariano Domingo," Bellamy continued. "An antiquarian who wore the mask of a gentleman collector. He was tied to scholars, museums, and libraries throughout England. But what he gathered, he did not display. He hoarded it, pieces of the old world locked away, waiting for the Brotherhood's purposes."

Primrose's mind flashed to her own shelves of rare books, suddenly unsure which pages might conceal Information like his.

"And—" Bellamy said "Edmund Ashcroft, He owned the daily in Haworth."

The name struck her like a blow. He has to be Rowan's father.

"I'll spare you the details of their demise," he whispered.

Bellamy's face was solemn. He let the words fall into the quiet of their surroundings.

Bellamy's eyes softened, though his voice carried the weight of warning. "Primrose... your father confided more in Athena than in any mortal man. That bird knows things I could never tell you. Watch her. Trust her instincts. She will lead you when the trail seems lost."

Primrose glanced toward the compass, its jeweled face glinting faintly. "And the compass?" she asked.

"Keep it hidden," he said firmly. "If the Brotherhood learns it is in your possession, they will tear this world apart to reclaim it."

Her fingers brushed the spine of the poetry book resting on the table. "And what of this book?"

Bellamy's face darkened. He exhaled slowly, heavily. "It has begun. You are already being watched. They are going to test you, reminding you that they see, that they know."

A chill slid down Primrose's spine.

"You should not linger here," Bellamy continued. He pushed the book gently back toward her, his eyes flicking once again to the limestone crags as if expecting shadows there. "I will contact you when it is safe. I trust you met my sister at the inn?"

"Yes." She said. "I put It together, it seemed she already knew me."

"She was expecting you 'tis true." He smiled, "Your father was one for making plans that were ironclad."

Primrose's throat tightened. "And you?"

He gave a weary half-smile. "I've spent my life

running just ahead of their fire. It will not be the first time I vanish into the smoke. But you—" his gaze sharpened, urgent "—you must go. Tonight. Don't linger here. I know a man in Settle who will take you back discretely."

Primrose gathered her things in her satchel.

"Thank you," she whispered.

Bellamy walked her out of the tent and asked her, "Do you ride?" as he motioned to the horses.

She smiled and said not since I was a child, but I'll give It a go!"

Thaddeus and Primrose rode back to the town taking trails that few people use. Near the river, In the cover of the trees, the stopped the horses.

"Gather your things at the inn and meet me back here." He said.

"Be careful, Primrose," he said, voice low and steady. "The Brotherhood hunts in shadows, but you are your father's daughter. And that may be our one hope yet."

Primrose discreetly went to her room and gathered her belongings. She slipped out of the inn unnoticed and made her way back to the river.

She found Dr. Bellamy waiting there for her with another man who had a covered carriage.

He was a hell built younger man, with dark brown hair and striking blue eyes. The carriage was black, solid, and had hand painted text in white paint on the side that read: Farrier Service.

"Primrose, this is one of my students, Leo, his father is a farrier, and this carriage will hide you nicely." said Thaddeus.

"Come love, let me help you up." Leo said as he offered his hand to her.

"Keep her safe Leo." Bellamy said.

"I will." Said the young man.

"Leo Is It? Primrose tried to make conversation as she rode in the back of the carriage, a small window between them.

"Yes miss." he said.

"How did you come to be Thadde—I mean, Dr. Bellamy's student?"

"Funny that." Leo said. "His horse threw a shoe, and my father was working on his horse when I met 'im. He was telling a story about what they found in the cave, and I wanted to see it and be a part of it, so he said he'd teach me. I owe 'im."

They carried on like that as they travelled. When they reached the forest near Haworth, Leo slowed the carriage and listened for anyone nearby.

After a good while, he went to the carriage door and said, "All looks to be quiet love."

"Thank you," Primrose said as she stepped down, her satchel heavy at her side, her mind still crowded with Bellamy's words.

She waved as he drew the carriage away slowly as quietly as they arrived.

Making her way through the trees with the borrowed lamp from the farrier's cart, she reached the familiar cobbled street near the inn and extinguished her lamp. The chill air icing her cheeks. She took a steadying breath—then froze.

A carriage stood waiting at the curb, its black body gleaming faintly in the lamplight. The driver tipped his hat, but it was not he who caught her breath.

The door swung open with a soft creak.

Inside, a face she knew regarded her steadily.

For a heartbeat, she hesitated—then, as if pulled by some invisible thread, she stepped forward and climbed inside.

The door shut behind her, the sound final, echoing in the hollow of her chest.

The carriage rocked gently as it rolled through the lamplit streets of Haworth. Primrose sat stiff-backed, her satchel clutched tightly in her lap. At last, she found her voice.

"Hello… Father."

17 HIGHER POWERS

The priest inclined his head with a gentle smile, though his eyes did not quite match it. "Miss Eversley. I heard chatter in town that you had gone to Settle. A long journey for a lady on her own. I thought it best to wait for you here, to see you safely home."

Primrose's brow furrowed. "And why should my safety concern you so deeply, Father? You are a man of the parish, not my guardian."

He folded his hands neatly in his lap, his voice calm. "Because, my dear, my role in this town is not quite what it appears. My name is Elias Hargrave."

Primrose gently pushed at her glasses that had slid down her nose. "Hargrave..."

He nodded once. "I am someone who—how shall I say this—keeps things in balance in this town. That is my only purpose here, despite what you may have heard in your travels. Whatever stories others may tell, know this: I answer to a higher power."

Shock and fear clutched at her chest, but she forced herself to meet his eyes. Her voice was thin, but stinging. "Did you... help Fenwick kill my father?"

"No," he said simply.

Her throat burned. "But you allowed it to happen?"

His gaze fell, and for the first time there was something like sorrow in it. "Yes."

Primrose's composure broke. Tears welled and spilled freely as she whispered, "Why?

The carriage wheels rattled to a halt. Outside, she saw the familiar outline of the bookshop against the night.

"This is your stop, my dear," Hargrave said quietly.

She lingered, trembling, her voice breaking as she

whispered again, "Why?"

He looked at her, his expression unreadable. "As I said—I must answer to a higher power."

Her eyes flared with sudden, desperate anger. "Fenwick?"

For the first time, his lips curved into something colder than a smile. He tipped his hat.

"Good night, Miss Eversley."

The door swung open, spilling lamplight across the cobblestones.

Primrose stood rooted on the cobblestones, tears streaming down her cheeks as the carriage wheels rattled away into the night. She watched until its shadowy form disappeared down the narrow street, toward the church spire that loomed black against the stars.

Her breath came in shuddering gasps. The priest's words clung to her like smoke—*I must answer to a higher power.*

At last, her knees trembling, she turned. She fumbled with the key, her fingers clumsy with cold and grief, then she dragged herself through the green wooden door of the shop. The door clicked shut, and she turned the lock with a final, decisive twist.

The silence of the bookshop closed around her. Familiar, steady. Only the faint rustle of pages shifting in a draft and the smell of leather and old paper.

Weary, she climbed the stairs to the living quarters. As she walked past her father's study, Athena stirred on her perch, amber eyes glinting in the moonlight. The owl gave a low, soft sound, as though in greeting.

Primrose's heart eased. Safe. At least here, with Athena, she felt safe.

She crossed the room, her body heavy, her spirit raw. Without undressing, she sank onto her bed. The sobs came once more, deep and wrenching, until exhaustion pulled her under.

By the time sleep claimed her, Athena had shifted closer, watching over her from the shadows with unblinking eyes.

The morning light crept pale and thin through the curtains, touching the edges of her bed. Primrose stirred, her body aching as though she had wrestled through the night with invisible hands.

The memories rushed back—Bellamy's confession, the priest's revelation, the carriage, the whispered higher power.

She sat up slowly, pressing her palms against her temples. She knew the truth now. Or enough of it to see the shape of the shadow pressing down on Haworth. But truth without proof was as fragile as ash. What could she take to the constable? A compass that spun toward secrets? A letter full of riddles? The word of a priest who admitted his guilt yet cloaked it in obedience to some unseen master?

No. None of it would stand in the light of day.

Helplessness threatened to swallow her. For a moment, she let herself feel it, the weight of her father's death, of enemies on every side, of being watched by eyes she could not see. Then she drew in a slow breath and pushed it down.

Helplessness was not the end. Determination would be her answer.

She rose and crossed to her desk, laying out the compass, the map, the poetry book, the acorn. Each piece was a fragment of her father's legacy, each a reminder that she was not yet finished. She traced her fingers across the compass, feeling its silent promise.

She would find evidence. She would gather the truth into something undeniable. And she would bring justice—not just for her father, but for every soul the Brotherhood sought to bend to its will.

Yet even as her resolve hardened, a shiver ran down her spine. She was being watched now. She could feel it, as keenly as if unseen eyes pressed against her window.

Her next steps would need to be chosen with care. One false move, and she would not live long enough to make another.

18 THE TOMB

Sunday quietly pressed around the shop like a hush in a church. Primrose padded across the creaking boards of her father's study, her fingertips brushing the spines of his journals. She had walked this room a dozen times since her return, yet today she forced herself to look with new eyes—determined, searching.

On the desk lay the familiar scatter of letters, scraps of paper, books, and the box. But it was the cabinet by the window that caught her attention. One drawer, slightly ajar, beckoned to her. With a tug it slid open, and inside, a bundle of papers waiting to be reviewed. *What clues will I find in her, Papa?*

They weren't just letters, they were overwritten drafts, each page filled with her father's careful script and then crossed through with darker ink. In the margins, he had various doodles, a spiral, a key, a flame, and a rune. It was as if he was writing his own manuscript. This will take some time, she thought to herself. Then she saw it.

Folded into the last sheet was something she hadn't noticed before a pressed sprig of rosemary, brittle but fragrant even now. Her father had underlined the word 'Remembrance' beside it.

What was he trying to make her remember? And why hide it in a pile of abandoned drafts? She felt more confused now than ever. She decided now would be a great time for tea and breakfast.

Athena fluttered from the study perch to her shoulder, then onward, gliding into the kitchen as if she, too, sensed the need for a pause. The bird settled atop the doorframe, tilting her head with a low, curious hiss.

Primrose busied herself with the familiar motions of tea and breakfast. The kettle went onto the hob, bread was sliced, eggs laid out beside rashers of bacon, and the scent of black pudding mingled with the sharp tang of tomatoes waiting to be grilled. A proper Sunday breakfast—her mother's breakfast.

As the kettle began its low whistle, a memory rose unbidden: her mother standing at the stove, sleeves rolled, humming a song under her breath. And always—always—the glint of her dragonfly comb pinning back her hair, wings etched so finely they seemed ready to take flight.

Primrose's gaze flicked upward. The porcelain bowl, painted with delicate flowers, still sat on the high kitchen shelf. Dust rimmed its lip, but it had remained untouched all these years. She reached up on tiptoe, pulled it down, and set it gently on the table. This Is where her mother kept the comb.

Inside it lay, just as she remembered—gleaming dragonfly wings spread wide. But tucked beneath it was something else: a small iron key, heavy for its size, cool against her palm.

Somehow, she knew, without knowing how, that this key belonged to another locked door in the chambers below. Her father must have hidden it here, waiting for the day she might remember.

Athena gave a sudden screech, feathers ruffling as if to say, 'let's go'.

Primrose closed her fingers around the key. Breakfast forgotten, tea cooling in the pot, her heart pounding.

The hidden chamber was full of doors. Which one would this open—and what truth waited on the other side?

The key bit into her palm as she hurried from the kitchen, her skirt swishing against her legs. There was no time to linger over tea. She bolted straight to her father's office where the jeweled compass and the carved wooden box rested on the desk. She opened It and grabbed the familiar yet mystical spiral key.

With careful hands she tucked the compass into her pocket and whispered to herself the steps she had taken before—as though repeating a ritual.

Athena swooped after her, silent but watchful, as they descended the spiral staircase. At the final step,

Primrose pressed her hand to the stair tread she knew to be loose.

A low groan of shifting stone answered. The stairs shuddered, then coiled downward like a corkscrew, unfurling into the dark below. A stale, earthy wind rose to greet her.

She reached for the lamp she had brought from her room—a glass oil lamp with a clear chimney, hastily filled and lit. Its flame bobbed uncertainly, casting pools of amber light that danced against the stone walls. Athena fluttered down the staircase.

The chamber stretched out in a narrow corridor lined with heavy wooden doors, each bound in iron. The silence was complete, broken only by the faint hiss of the lamp and the steady tick of the compass needle inside her pocket.

Primrose drew out the compass and the iron key. She held the compass and it just spun in circles.

Odd, it worked before.

She tried the first door—too large, the key didn't fit in lock. The second—again, no luck. At the third, the key slid in with startling ease.

Athena gave a sharp, approving screech.

Primrose swallowed, tightened her grip on the lamp, and slowly turned the key.

The lock clicked. The door shivered open a crack, exhaling a breath of air that smelled of perfumed flowers. The room was warm and cast in candlelight from large pillars of wax.

She pushed the door wider.

The door creaked open as it gave way. For a moment Primrose thought the room empty. Then the light caught on glass—an ornate oil lamp, set upon a pedestal. Its glass chimney was etched with vines and roses, the flame within burning steadily as though it had never known want of oil. The fire shimmered with a warmth too constant to be natural.

Her gaze shifted to the far wall. There, set into an arched recess framed with gilded scrollwork, rested an urn. The nameplate gleamed in the lamplight: Elizabeth Eversley.

Her knees weakened. *Mother.*

She moved closer, hand trembling as she brushed the dust from the polished silver. A yellowed clipping lay propped against the base: Funeral Services for Mrs.

Elizabeth Eversley Held at St. Mark's Church in-the-Bowery in the East Village, New York, New York.

A sob rose in her throat. She was back in that candle lit chapel, the scent of lilies pressing heavy in the air. She remembered clutching her handkerchief, searching the mourners' faces, waiting for her father to appear. But he had never come. Days later, she had stood by the grave that the funeral director assured her held her mother's body. She had wept there, believing the earth cradled her at last.

Yet here are her ashes—hidden all these years.

Her father had brought her mother home.

The weight of it broke her. She fell to her knees, pressing her hand against the urn, forehead bowed. The tears came hot and unrelenting, wracking sobs that seemed to echo against the stone walls. Athena gave a soft, mournful hiss from her perch on a single chair that her father must have sat in many times, grieving with her.

At last, when her breath steadied, Primrose rose again. She wiped her cheeks with her sleeve, the ache in her chest sharper but strangely solid, as if grief itself had reforged her spine.

The lamplight flickered across a series of nine portraits hung on the opposite wall. Faces of men stared back: some stern, others smiling, all painted with the formal precision of the Edwardian style. One face seized her: Harold Fenwick.

Pinned at the frame's edge was a folded letter.

Hands shaking, she opened it. Her father's hand.

My dearest daughter,

If you are reading this, then my fears have come to pass. These portraits line the wall so you may know who your enemies are, and to keep you safe. The evidence of my own death will not be easy to find—the Brotherhood leaves no trace. But your mother's death, though disguised as an accident, is the thread you must follow. Her urn rests here, but her death points directly to Fenwick.

I could not pursue it myself, for fear they would kill you as they killed her. But you, my daughter, are stronger than you know. Enclosed is the signed confession of the buggy driver who struck her down. Deliver it to Constable Grant. You may trust him; he is not corrupt like the rest. He will investigate it quietly.

Do not speak of it to others.

There is one more task I beg of you. Should I fall, I instructed Reverend Hargrave to see that my own body be cremated, and my ashes kept safe. Seek him and obtain them. He will understand. Place my ashes here beside your beloved mother. And when you do, you will see that my choices, though flawed, were made only to shield you from this darkness.

Forgive me for the deceptions, for the silence, for leaving you in the shadows. You are old enough now to know the truth, and perhaps strong enough to finish what I could not. Carry the light forward, Primrose.

Your loving father,

Alaric Eversley

Primrose's grip on the letter tightened. Her mother—murdered. Her father—hunted. Fenwick—and others.

The chamber closed around her like a tomb, but within her breast the flame of resolve burned brighter than the eternal lamp.

The portraits on the wall stared down like silent accusers, each face a reminder of the danger pressing in. Grief still pulled at her ribs, yet within her heart, the flame of resolve flared hotter. She would take the confession to Constable Grant. She would confront the truths her father had hidden. And though the letter bade her to trust Hargrave, the thought made her blood run cold. If her father had tied his last request to that man, then she would need to tread carefully indeed.

She lowered the letter with trembling hands and turned, noticing for the first time the single chair positioned before the portraits. Its wood was dark and worn smoothly at the arms, as though her father had sat there often, pondering these faces, searching for the thread that tied them together.

Primrose eased into the seat. The cushion sagged beneath her, faintly scented with dust and the ghost of pipe smoke. She closed her eyes, imagining her father hunched forward in this very place, candlelight flickering over his features as he pieced together the fragments of betrayal, desperation burning in his chest, grief gnawing at his soul.

How many nights had he sat in silence, staring at Fenwick's painted face, knowing the man was responsible yet powerless to bring him to justice? How heavy had the secret weighed, keeping her safe while abandoning his own chance at justice or vengeance?

Her hand drifted to the arm of the chair, fingers tracing the worn groove. A whisper of connection stirred—father and daughter, both seated in judgment of the same shadows.

"I will finish it for you," she breathed, voice breaking into the stillness. "For both of you."

Athena answered with a soft, solemn hiss, as if to seal the vow.

Her gaze returned to the urn, the nameplate gleaming in the lamplight. The grief it stirred pulled her back to the day of the funeral, the chapel heavy with lilies, the murmur of hymns, and her own small hands trembling against a black dress too big for her frame.

She remembered standing at the graveside, lost and frightened, when her uncle, her mother's brother, bent low and whispered, "Everything will be all right, little one. I will watch over you always." His arms had been strong, steady, a promise against the chaos that had swallowed her world.

In the months and years that followed, he had kept that promise. His household had become her own. His wife had treated her like a daughter; his children, like a sister. He had guided her education, encouraged her love of books, and celebrated every success as if she were born of his own blood.

Tears pricked her eyes anew, not only from sorrow but from gratitude. For all that had been taken from her, she had been given him—a guardian, a father in all but name.

She stood, walked over to the shrine in the wall, brushed her fingertips once more across her mother's urn, whispering, "You would be glad to know I was never truly alone. Thank you for naming Uncle Bjorn as my guardian."

Athena shifted on her perch, feathers rustling softly, as though reminding her that even blessings could cast long shadows.

Primrose turned to look over her shoulder, meeting Athena's wide, amber eyes glinting in the lamplight. The owl gave a slow, deliberate blink, as though weighing what had been spoken.

19 THE EVIDENCE

With the letter folded carefully into her pocket, Primrose stood and cast one last look about the chamber. The eternal lamp glowed softly, its light steady as a heartbeat. The urn rested untouched, her mother's presence both comfort and sorrow. She could not bear to close the door on her again.

Instead, she left the lock turned open, the passage breathing quietly behind her. The secrets were no longer hidden—they were hers to guard.

Before she turned to leave, her gaze returned to the portraits. Three of the men stared down from the wall: Fenwick, and two others their names revealed to her by Dr. Thaddeus Bellamy. Their painted eyes seemed to follow her. With sudden firmness she stepped to the wall, lifted the frames from their hooks, and tucked them under her arm. They would no longer hang in silence down here. Two down, Fenwick, but who are these other six men?

Athena glided after her as she made her way back through the corridor, up the spiral staircase, and into the familiar hush of the bookshop above.

She then carried the evidence upstairs and placed it on the desk, the portraits she tossed in the fire and watched them burn with a stoic look on her face.

The desk now looked less like a scholar's workspace and more like a tribunal table, each scrap of evidence demanding judgment.

Her shoulders sagged with sudden weariness. She had not yet eaten. With a sigh, she turned toward the kitchen. Tea still waited to be poured, bacon and bread to be fried, eggs to be set upon the pan. A proper breakfast—her mother's Sunday breakfast—would steady her hands and clear her thoughts for what must come next.

And she missed her so much she needed that comforting meal.

By mid-morning, Primrose made her way up the cobbled street to St. Michael's, the stone church's bell tolled faithfully over Haworth. Townsfolk filed in with their hymnals and Sunday best, exchanging nods and murmured greetings. She slipped into a pew midway down the nave.

From the pulpit, Reverend Hargrave raised his eyes—and for the briefest moment, they locked with hers. His gaze was level, unreadable, yet it held her long enough that her heart gave a hard, warning thump. She lowered her eyes and clasped her hands, as though in fervent prayer.

The sermon that morning was telling. Hargrave spoke of sin concealed, and secrets brought to light, of false shepherds among the flock, of the wages of silence. His words rang through the vaulted space, weighted and deliberate. Primrose sat stiff-backed, trying to commit every phrase to memory. Each line felt aimed, not at the congregation at large, but at her.

She wondered whether anyone else heard the warning beneath his tone—or if she alone recognized the double edge of his scripture.

Primrose lingered after the final hymn faded and the congregation shuffled out, murmuring in clusters at the doors. She remained seated, hands folded in her lap, eyes fixed on the polished wood of the pew before her. At last, the church grew quiet. Only the shuffle of steps echoed as Reverend Hargrave returned from greeting parishioners, moving slowly back toward the altar.

When his gaze found her still waiting, his brows rose faintly. He approached, slid into the pew beside her, and folded his hands.

Her voice was barely above a whisper. "Do you have my father's ashes?"

"Yes." His tone was even, unshaken. He inclined his head slightly. "Come with me."

She stood, skirt brushing the floor, and followed as he led her down a side aisle toward the vestry. They moved into a narrow corridor, its stone walls cool and damp. She expected him to stop at his office, the plain door with its wood nameplate loomed just ahead—but he walked past without pause. She cast it a sidelong glance, confusion tugging at her features, then hurried after him.

Further along, they came to a tall oak door banded with iron, its hinges blackened with age. Hargrave drew a key from his pocket, heavy and ornate, and fit it into the lock. With a groan of iron, the door swung open.

Warm lamp light spilled into the hall. She stepped inside. Shelves rose from floor to ceiling, lined with scrolls, worn books, and curious artifacts glinting in the flickering glow. The air was thick with the scent of old parchment and beeswax.

At the center of the room, upon a carved pedestal, stood a beautiful urn—polished bronze chased with silver vines, its surface gleaming as though freshly burnished.

Primrose froze, her heart beating hard. She had found hidden chambers beneath her father's shop, but this... this secret room in the church told its own story.

Hargrave stepped to the pedestal, his expression solemn. He grasped the urn with both hands, lifting it as though it weighed more than metal and ash, and turned to her.

"This is what he entrusted to me," he said quietly, placing it carefully into her arms. The bronze was cool against her palms, the engraved vines catching the lamplight.

"He will be at peace now."

Primrose's head snapped up. "How do you know?"

"Because you know the truth," Hargrave replied, his voice steady, eyes fixed on hers with unsettling calm.

She felt desperately tried to catch her breath, startled at his certainty, at the implication that he had been waiting for this very moment. Her grip tightened around the urn. "Why did my father trust you?"

Hargrave's lips curved in something that was neither quite a smile nor a frown. "Because he understood what I keep in balance."

"Because he understood what I keep in balance."

Primrose searched his face, heart thudding. The urn felt heavy in her arms. "Can I trust you?" she asked softly.

For a long moment, he held her gaze. Then, instead

of answering, Hargrave's smile deepened—enigmatic, unreadable. With one hand, he gestured toward the open door.

The lamplight flickered as if stirred by an unseen draft, and the silence pressed in until she turned, clutching the urn, and stepped back into the corridor.

They walked in silence through the cloisters, their footsteps echoing against the cold stone. The air smelled faintly of wax and incense, the hush of the church settling over them like a shroud.

When they reached his office, Hargrave opened the door at last. From a cupboard he drew out a simple burlap sack and held it toward her. "Here," he said. "Let's not give away all our secrets."

Primrose slipped the urn carefully inside, the rough fibers scratching against the polished bronze. The bag concealed its gleam, but not its weight. She clutched it close, feeling the hidden burden press against her ribs.

At the church's great doors, she turned to leave. Hargrave lingered in the threshold, his expression unreadable in the shifting light of the nave.

"Psalm thirty-three," he said quietly.

She turned looking at him inquisitively.

"It will give you the peace you seek." He continued.

The words followed her out into the chill air, echoing like a benediction—or a warning.

The heavy church doors closed behind her with a hollow thud, and the world outside felt suddenly sharp and vivid. She drew her shawl tighter, the burlap sack clutched close beneath her arm, its rough weaves pressing against her palm.

The cobbled street glistened faintly from an earlier rain, carrying with it the scent of wet stone, peat, and the smoke drifting from nearby chimneys. Shop shutters rattled as merchants reopened after service, their voices rising in familiar greetings. A cart creaked past, iron wheels grinding over uneven stones, while a child tugged at his mother's hand, laughing, his boots splashing through shallow puddles.

Above it all the church bell tolled the hour, deep and resonant, carrying over the rooftops like a reminder she could not shake. *Psalm thirty-three. It will give you the peace you seek*. Hargrave's voice lingered in her ears, solemn and insistent.

Primrose inhaled, the damp air cool against her

cheeks. The moor wind whispered down the lanes, stirring the scent of heather and the faint sweetness of toffee from the confectioner's shop. She felt both grounded in the ordinary bustle of the village and strangely apart from it, as though the burlap sack in her arms marked her as set apart—keeper of a secret no one else could guess.

Her steps slowed as she reached the steep curve of Main Street. Each stone cottage seemed to watch her, windows glinting in the weak sun. She shifted the sack against her side, the urn's weight pressing steadily and inescapable.

By the time the worn brick of her father's bookshop came into view, her resolve had settled like a stone in her chest. The door with its green paint and trailing ivy looked as it always had, but she carried inside her something altogether changed—her father's ashes, her heartbreak, and a psalm she had yet to read.

Back inside the shop, Primrose set the burlap sack on the countertop and began to search the shelves. Her fingertips skimmed leather spines until at last she drew out a heavy volume—an illuminated Bible, its cover worn but dignified, the pages edged in gilt. When she opened it briefly, the script gleamed, framed by painted vines and angels, a work of art as much as devotion.

She cradled it against her side, gathered the sack with the urn, and paused by the door. Outside, the rosemary pots trembled in the breeze, blue blossoms bright against their green stalks.

She set her treasures down for a moment and stepped outside. She clipped a vaseful, their fragrance sharp and comforting. She locked the shop's door and then carried all three—Bible, sack, and flowers—down the winding stair once more. Athena followed, her wings whispering softly in the air.

The chamber welcomed her with its lamplight and silence. She crossed to the shrine in the wall, setting the burlap sack down gently. With reverent care she drew out her father's urn and placed it beside her mother's.

The two vessels, bronze and silver, gleamed together at last.

In the center she placed the vase of blooming rosemary, the blossoms nodding like witnesses between them. The scent filled the chamber, clean and sweet, winding through the still air.

She stepped back, then turned toward the chair and sank into it. The Bible lay heavy on her lap as she opened to the marked *Psalms*, fingers trembling slightly as the pages fanned past illuminated capitals and curling vines of ink.

At last, she found the number she sought. Psalm 33.

She drew in a steadying breath, the urns and rosemary before her, Athena rustling softly above, and began to read.

Her voice trembled at first, then steadied as she read aloud:

"Sing joyfully to the Lord, you righteous;
It is fitting for the upright to praise him.
Praise the Lord with the harp;
make music to him on the ten-stringed lyre.
Sing to him a new song;
play skillfully and shout for joy."

The words lingered in the still air, echoing faintly against the chamber's stone walls. As she spoke them, she felt the heaviness of grief loosen, as though unseen hands had gently lifted it from her shoulders. A hush fell over her spirit, not empty, but tender and consoling.

For a fleeting moment she heard music in her mind—a harp's clear strings, a lyre's low hum—tones weaving with her own voice until it seemed she was not reading alone but joining a chorus long established.

She lowered her gaze again to the page, heart thudding with quiet awe, and found her place at the psalm's close. Her lips shaped the final words, steady and sure:

"May your unfailing love be with us, Lord,
even as we put our hope in you."

The flame of the eternal lamp flickered as though in response, and the rosemary's fragrance deepened, filling the chamber with a living sweetness. Primrose closed her eyes, letting the verse settle in her chest like a promise.

Primrose lingered in the chamber, sitting in stillness as though the stone itself invited her into meditation. The rosemary's fragrance hung in the air, mingling with the low burn of the eternal flame. Time seemed to fold—minutes or hours, she could not tell.

At last, she rose. Carefully she closed the Bible and left it upon the chair. One final glance at the twin urns and the vase of blossoms, and she turned, Athena gliding silently behind her, and made her way back upstairs.

In the main room of her quarters she sank onto the couch, still cradled in silence. Fatigue swept over her like a tide. She laid down and let her eyes wander the familiar room, her gaze unfocused, drifting.

Then she saw it.

Against the far wall stood a shape she had somehow overlooked before a U-shaped frame with two arms supporting a crossbar, from which strings stretched taut to a polished soundbox.

Her breath caught. It can't be.

She sat upright, staring. *An artifact, in plain sight.* The very words from her father's notes whispered back to her now. A lyre—an ancient instrument, here, under her own roof.

Hargrave's voice echoed in her mind: Psalm thirty-three... The very psalm that spoke of the harp and the lyre. Had he known? Had he meant for her to see it?

Primrose rose slowly. She reached out, fingertips brushing the strings, a faint vibration trembling into the air. Where would this lead? To Fenwick, somehow—her father's letter had tied her mother's death to him, and the psalm, the lyre, it all pointed forward.

The path was narrowing. And Fenwick waited at its end.

20 FENWICK'S GIFT

The morning light fell pale across the shop windows as Primrose turned the lock and let Maggie inside. The girl's cheeks were flushed from the walk, auburn curls escaping her bonnet as she bustled in.

"Thought I might tidy the shelves this morning," Maggie offered brightly.

"Wonderful" Primrose said. "I must go to see the constable this morning. I shall be back shortly."

Primrose managed a thin smile. "After you've finished tidying things, I'd like you to look through my father's inventory." She said tapping the stack of books on the counter. "See if you can find which artifacts have been sold, and which remain. I need to know precisely what we have, starting with this lyre."

Maggie's face lit at the responsibility. "Yes, I can manage this." she said as she paused and reached for the feather duster.

As Maggie went about tidying the shop, Primrose grabbed her shawl and made her way out into the town.

Constable Grant smiled at Primrose as she walked into his office. His steady eyes gave him an air of unshakable patience.

When she laid the papers on his desk, and said, "I've something urgent for you." His expression hardened but not with surprise. He leaned back in his chair, fingers steepled.

"I've been waiting for you, Miss Eversley," he said quietly.

She looked puzzled. "Waiting?"

He nodded. "Your father said if you ever came with evidence in hand, it would mean his work had ended and yours had begun."

"His work?" she asked.

He stood, walked to the office door, glanced out at the bobbies walking about, then shut the door.

When he sat back down, he leaned in and said, "Miss Eversley, I keep things in line in this town, but I answer to a higher power."

For the next hour, Grant discussed the suspicious accident that claimed her mother and the Brotherhood's reach. "Your father was right," he said grimly. "As a rule, they leave no trace. But this—" he held up the confession— "this is enough to hang Fenwick on the charge of murder."

Primrose felt a strange blend of grief and relief. "Then you will arrest him?"

"Aye." Grant rose from his desk, buckling his coat. "At once."

Primrose straightened. "Then I'll go with you. I want to see Fenwick brought to justice."

He shook his head firmly. "No. This is work for the bobbies; it's too be dangerous. There's no place in it for a lady. You'll return to your shop and wait. When he is in custody, I'll send word to you."

Her lips pressed tight, indignation sparking, "But I insist."

"Dammit lass, are you not listening to me?" He barked at Primrose. "It's too bloody dangerous."

"I can't go on worrying about you and him and my men at the same time. Bloody hell." He said exacerbated.

She gave him a shrewd look, and he put his hands up and apologized.

"Miss Eversley, Primrose, I can't keep you safe."

And with that a sadness in his face betrayed him and she knew what he meant.

She gathered her shawl and let Grant lead her to the door. He tipped his hat. "Courage, Miss Eversley. Justice will find its way."

Constable Grant rode at the front of the carriage,

two bobbies beside him armed with .455 Webley revolvers and truncheons. The wheels jolted over ruts as they made their way along the narrow lane, the oak tree looming larger with every turn.

"There it is," Grant said grimly, pointing with his truncheon.

The carriage rattled to a halt before the weathered wooden door, its iron fittings dark with age. The men disembarked, boots striking the ground in a chorus. revolvers were drawn, truncheons at the ready. Grant raised his voice, the sound carrying across the quiet countryside.

"Harold Fenwick! In the King's name, come out and surrender yourself!"

The wind stirred through the branches of the oak. No answer came.

"Once more!" Grant barked. "Fenwick! Step out, or we'll come in after you!"

Again, silence. Only the creak of the great tree and the distant caw of a crow broke the stillness.

Grant motioned to his men. "On me."

Two shouldered the door. The old wood easily gave way. Pistols raised, the party surged inside.

The rooms yawned empty before them. No fire burned in the hearth, no coat hung by the peg. Dust drifted lazily in the daylight, settling over bare floorboards. Fenwick had gone, and gone thoroughly—no papers, no food, not even a candle left behind.

Grant lowered his revolver, jaw tightening. "He's slipped through our hands in the night."

The men muttered, some swore under their breath. One of the deputies kicked at the cold ashes in the hearth, scattering gray flakes across the stone.

Grant's voice was hard. "Search it top to bottom. Every nook, every beam."

But as the lanterns probed each corner, the truth became plain: Harold Fenwick had vanished without a trace.

Footsteps on the floorboards caused the men to all turn.

Rowan Ashcroft emerged from the empty doorway.

"So, it's true, then," he murmured. "Fenwick's flown."

Grant gave a gruff nod. "Slippery sort, but he'll not

stay hidden forever."

Rowan pulled out his notebook. "The people will need to hear it. Best they know the truth."

Two days later, the Haworth Gazette carried Rowan's article: *Local Merchant Implicated in Murder, Now Missing Without a Trace*. His words spread quickly, retold in the bakery, the mill, the inn. Fenwick's name became both scandal and legend.

And at the little bookshop on Main Street, curiosity bloomed. Customers came not only for the promise of rare tomes but to glimpse the place at the center of the town's great mystery. They whispered among the shelves, casting sidelong looks at Primrose as though she were a heroine from one of her shop's books.

Primrose, standing at the counter, she felt it was now safe to let Athena perch nearby. She felt the weight of her father's legacy more keenly than ever. Justice for them both remained unfinished. Fenwick was still out there. But the path forward was clear, and she would walk it—step by step, clue by clue.

That evening, the rain had settled into a steady patter against the windows. A lamp glowed warmly on her father's desk, illuminating the growing pile of papers, maps, and portraits that marked the course of her days since arriving.

Primrose dipped her pen into the inkwell, hesitating only a moment before setting it to the page.

To the Board of Trustees, she wrote in her careful, measured hand. *It is with deep gratitude and no small measure of regret that I tender my resignation from my position at the Astor Library in Manhattan. My circumstances have changed in ways I could never have foreseen, and my path now lies here, in Haworth, at the bookshop my father entrusted to me. I hope you will understand my decision.*

She set the pen aside, watching the ink glisten before it dried. The words felt strange, as though they belonged to someone else. Yet when she signed her name—*Primrose Eversley*—a quiet certainty settled in her chest. For the first time, she was *choosing* to stay.

The evening stilled around her; the silence broken only by the ticking of the clock and Athena's occasional rustle from her perch. Weariness pressed down, and she allowed herself to recline, eyes drifting across the familiar contours of the room.

Her gaze lingered on the newly discovered lyre, its strings glinting in the lamp's glow.

A sudden knock shattered the stillness.

It echoed through the shop—firm, insistent—jarring her. Athena's wings flared wide as she gave a sharp cry.

Primrose said to herself, *"It's well past dusk. Who could possibly be calling now?"*

The knock came again, sharper this time. Primrose rose and descended the stairs, lamp in hand. She could see a messenger through the glass of the shop door. She unlatched it just enough to see a boy standing there in a messenger's cap, his boots splattered with mud.

"Miss Primrose Eversley?" he asked.

"Yes," she said cautiously.

He held out a small parcel wrapped in brown paper and tied with twine. "I have a package for you."

Her brow furrowed. "From whom?"

The boy glanced at the tag. "Name says... Harold Fenwick."

Primrose held her breath for a brief second, her eyes widening. "Fenwick?"

The boy nodded, unfazed. "Need your mark here, miss."

Her hand trembled as she signed the slip. The messenger tipped his cap, pressed the package into her hands, and vanished down the street.

She shut the door swiftly, turned the bolt, and leaned against it, the parcel heavy and strange in her hand. Then, with Athena swooping down to perch on the stair rail, she carried it upstairs to the living quarters.

She set it before her on the table, and took a seat,

staring at the plain wrapping as though it might leap to life. Her pulse thudded in her ears. Slowly, she tugged the twine free, peeled away the paper, and revealed a folded note.

Your father would want you to have this.

Beneath it lay a small key of carved green jade, its surface smooth, with ancient characters etched into the shank.

Primrose's breath quickened. A new mystery lay before her—left in her hands by the man who had murdered her parents, vanished without a trace, and now reached out from the shadows.

She sat back, the key glowing in the lamplight, and whispered to herself, "Why this... and why now?"

Athena gave a sharp cry, as though in answer.

She took the jade key and studied its carved dragon bow. As it rested in her palm, heavy with secrets, she knew the next chapter of her father's hidden world was waiting to be unraveled.

ACKNOWLEDGEMENTS

I want to thank my husband, Doug, who made it possible for me to truly pursue my dreams. I love you so much.

ABOUT THE AUTHOR

I'm Raynie—former journalist and editor (eighteen years in the trenches of deadlines and red pens), now a full-time cozy-mystery author and author-success coach. Reporting taught me to notice what other people miss; editing taught me how to shape a story so readers can't put it down. I use both every day as I write mysteries with gentle stakes, clever puzzles, and a touch of old-world magic. Between chapters, I coach writers through RLA Publishing, where I blend craft feedback, practical publishing strategy, and mindset support to help authors finish stronger and launch smarter.

When I'm not working, you'll find me haunting used-bookstores, tending to my garden, or researching strange historical footnotes that inevitably become plots. If you like botanicals, bookshops, and brave heroines, you're in the right place.

Thank you for venturing into Primrose Eversley's world. Your curiosity brought the shop to life and turned quiet pages into clues. I'm grateful you chose to spend some time in Haworth. Thank you for the time, the trust, and the turning of one more page. I can't wait to meet you at the next case. May your own compass keep pointing to wonder.
With gratitude,
Raynie Taylor

www.raynietaylor.com

www.rlapublishing.com

YOUR VOICE MATTERS

Dear Reader,
Thank you for stepping through the green door and spending time in Primrose Eversley's world. If this mystery kept you turning pages, would you leave a quick review? Just a sentence or two—and a star rating—will help other readers discover the series and tell the store algorithms this book is worth spotlighting.

You can review my book here (choose one—or all, if you're feeling extra kind!):
Amazon: https: https://tr.ee/8lAd5m
Goodreads: https: https://tr.ee/EG8wwE
Barnes and Noble: https://tr.ee/ZQpHfL

Thank you for reading—and for helping this indie author keep the bookshop lights on. I'll keep a lamp in the window for your next visit to Haworth.

With gratitude,
Raynie Andrewsen
Author of the Primrose Eversley Mysteries

Male catkin
Female flower
The Nut
The Cup

Quercus velutina

161

Book Club
Reader's Guide

Compass of Secrets

Raynie Taylor

Step into Primrose Eversley's world—tea optional, curiosity required. This *Compass of Secrets* Reading Guide includes a short introduction, discussion questions, book club enhancement ideas, and a Q&A with author *Raynie Taylor*. The questions are meant to help your group dig into the mystery, the motives, and the moments between the clues—so your conversation is as satisfying as the final reveal. Happy reading, and welcome to Primrose's world!

INTRODUCTION

Welcome to The Compass of Secrets book club guide! These questions and activities are designed to spark lively discussion about Primrose Eversley's journey, what she uncovers, what she risks, and what the jeweled compass reveals along the way. Whether your group loves picking apart clues, debating motives, or soaking in the atmosphere of the bookshop and its locked rooms, I hope this guide helps you dig deeper and enjoy the adventure even more.

DISCUSSION QUESTIONS

1. First impressions: What was your initial read on Primrose in the opening chapters? Did your opinion of her shift by the end?

2. The compass as a "character": The jeweled compass points to clues rather than a person— what does that choice add to the mystery? Did it change how you read the story?

3. Curiosity vs. caution: When did Primrose's curiosity feel brave—and when did it feel reckless? Which choice of hers did you most agree (or disagree) with?

4. The bookstore's secrets: What did the locked rooms/hidden materials in the shop symbolize to you—grief, legacy, power, identity, something else?

5. Grief and inheritance: How does Primrose's grief shape her decisions? What does she "inherit" beyond objects?

6. Trust and deception: Who did you trust the most early on—and who surprised you? What tipped you off (or misled you)?

7. Clues and misdirection: What clue felt the most important in hindsight? Which detail seemed small at first but became a turning point?

8. Moral gray areas: Did anyone do the "wrong thing" for the "right reason"? How did you feel about that choice?

9. Setting and mood: How does the setting (the town, the shop, the back rooms, the atmosphere) influence the tension and pacing?

10. Legacy and hidden lives: What does the book suggest about the stories people keep hidden, especially across generations?

11. Power and knowledge: Who holds power in this story, and why? Is it tied to information, money, fear, reputation, or something else?

12. The ending: Did the conclusion satisfy you emotionally and as a mystery? What would you have changed, if anything?

13. Looking ahead: What questions do you still have? What do you most want to see explored next in Primrose's world?

IDEAS TO ENHANCE YOUR BOOK CLUB'S EXPERIENCE

1. Clue Board Night: Bring sticky notes and make a simple "case board"—characters, motives, key clues, red herrings, and timeline. Vote on your top suspect halfway through, then revisit after the reveal.

2. Primrose's Playlist + Tea Pairing: Create a short playlist that fits the book's mood (mysterious, cozy, tense, vintage). Pair it with tea + a simple snack "fit for the bookshop" (shortbread, scones, jam, citrus cake).

QUESTIONS FOR THE AUTHOR

1. What was the first image, idea, or "spark" that made you want to write Primrose's story—and when did the compass enter the picture?

   "My mother-in-law was talking with me about cozy mysteries, and I started thinking about how cool it would be to mix genres using cozy mystery and fantasy. That was the spark that got me going and I knew If I was going to have a protagonist, she'd need to be a very Virgo type woman, so I made her a librarian. The compass came into the picture when I started thinking of Indiana Jones meets Primrose Eversley. She needed to have artifacts and curiosities in her life to make things interesting."

2. Which scene was the most difficult to write—and which was the most fun?

   "The most difficult scene to write was anytime she is interacting with Rowan Ashcroft because I didn't want their relationship to move too fast or too slow. I want to keep the tension between them, and we'll see where that leads in the next book. The most fun I had was writing the scene where she discovers the hidden chambers."

3. If readers take away one feeling or idea from The Compass of Secrets, what do you hope it is?

   "I hope that readers can take away that even when you experience great loss, you have it in you to carry on, be brave, and start your life anew-- even if that means in a new place you call home."

BOOK TWO COVER REVEAL

A PRIMROSE EVERSLEY MYSTERY
BOOK 2

The Temple Key

RAYNIE TAYLOR

COMING IN 2026